BURNING TIMBER

The Timberton Lake Series: Book One

Baynns M. Finnleigh

Bilmarlin Book Group
Nashua NH

To Mom
Your strength, wisdom and love carried us all.
You were an angel on earth as you are in heaven.
I love you and miss you.

CHAPTER ONE

She was an Ivy League law school graduate, top of her class. As one of New York City's most sought-after attorneys she had seen it all and wasn't afraid of anything. Except these numbers: 337-555-4411.

The message left on Madison's voicemail shook her steady disposition and derailed her laser focus from the legal brief she'd drafted in preparation for next week's court appearance.

When Detective Hanoy from her hometown of Timberton, Louisiana called several times a year, she felt compelled to respond, a familiar reaction to his phone number that sent a wave of nausea straight to the pit of her cast-iron stomach.

Time ticked away faster than the torrential rain that fell from the New York City sky outside her office window on the stormy Friday afternoon. Madison's paralegal lodged her head in the three-inch space between the frame and her office door.

"Madison, would you mind if I headed out a little early? The wind is really picking up out there. I'm sure it will blow my skirt clear over my head." Her signature laugh ended in its customary snort.

"Of course. Thank you for all your good work this week. Enjoy your weekend and we'll see you on Monday."

"You too, boss. I'll fill you in on my first date with this new guy I met online." She whipped her head out of the crevice, a hair follicle or two left behind.

Madison looked at the weather report as a perfect opportunity to duck out of the office early and head home to return the detective's call from the privacy of her apartment. She dialed Attorney Richard Connelly's extension.

"Richard, it's Madison. You're going to have to fly solo on the last two meetings you set up this afternoon. Explain later."

Most employees at the prestigious law firm of Branson, Scapatti and Boles would rearrange their life to attend a meeting scheduled by the great Richard Connelly, but the fact that he was Madison's longtime boyfriend meant she was uniquely qualified to display her independence and remind him to check his inflamed ego at the door at night.

The nor'easter that ravaged most of New England barreled down on the city. The ferocious storm packed fierce winds and golf ball-size hail. Social media enthusiasts posted photos of street signs blown off at every block and rows of fancy cars shot by bullets made of rubble.

Madison called the concierge in the lobby of her apartment building to send a car to pick her up at the office.

"Quite a storm we're having today, Miss Pike." The Canto Ricco Tower's most trusted driver engaged in his customary small talk as he pulled the car to the curb of her luxury residence.

"Crazy weather. Be safe. See you on Monday, 8:00 a.m. sharp." She handed him three crisp fifty-dollar bills and stepped onto the wet sidewalk.

"Thank you, ma'am." Not sure if the new bills stuck together or if she meant to hand him all three, he opened his driver's side window to get her attention. "This is very generous of you. Are you sure you meant to—"

"Yes, please take it. You deserve more. It's treacherous out here." She turned toward the entrance and ran into the building before she got swept up like a piece of debris.

The Canto Ricco stood firm and proud on its foundation. Madison and Richard's stature fit right in with its reputation for catering to the powerful elite.

Madison ran into the palatial lobby and shook the ice pellets off her umbrella. Her sexy smile greeted the door attendant, a smile he looked forward to every morning and every night.

The ornate, gold-plated elevator waited to carry her up to the 35th floor.

As Madison exited the elevator, there stood the last person she wanted to see.

"Hey there, Maddie." Buck, who lived down the hall but was always near her front door, pounced. "Looks like the weather roughed you up, you poor pretty little thang," he said with a twang, his forefinger pointed to her soaked, icy hair and her drenched designer coat.

"Yes, I suppose it did." She picked at the frozen pellets that managed to stick to the fine threads. "My umbrella provided no defense."

"No pun intended," he said with a failed attempt at a wink.

In her haze, it took her a moment to process his flirtatious banter. "Ah, yes. No defense." She addressed his so-called wit with a nod.

As Buck entered the elevator like he had just made some kind of brilliant exchange, he bowed to her and ended the encounter with one last wink. Annoyed to the point of no return, she flashed a half-smile and fought the temptation to use her umbrella to wipe the smirk off his face.

Buck's desire to bed Maddie was no secret to her, Richard, or anyone else in the building. Richard never saw Buck as a credible threat. Buck's advances were so lame they provided him with some welcome entertainment. In Richard's mind, no one was a threat. Except for one man, the only other man who ever owned a piece of Maddie's heart. Jordan Kingston.

Madison's history with Jordan nearly ended any chance of building a life with Richard. Her early attempts at honesty failed. Richard's temper rose to dangerous levels whenever she mentioned *his* name.

The truth could not be told without Jordan in it. It revolved around him. He remained in the center. Her center. All roads led back to him. If she wanted Richard, she had to lie to him, and to herself.

Desperate to propel her new life forward, she kept the truth locked up in a brown, cedar hope chest at the foot of her bed. Despite Richard's arrogant, self-absorbed ways, the good in him outweighed the bad. Most of the time. And even though history showed his inability to commit to one woman, this six-foot-four specimen of physical perfection was hers.

Keys in hand, Maddie unlocked the door to the sprawling, five thousand square foot luxury condo she'd bought with Richard last year. Her two most precious family members, Judge and Jury, her affectionate Golden Retriever puppies, jumped on her soaked attire and captured the dangling frozen ice pellets with their well-groomed fur.

"You two never can wait one minute, can you?" She rubbed the top of their furry heads and talked in a baby voice that calmed them.

"Hi, Shelby," Maddie said as she dodged a string of puddles courtesy of her pups. Her voice bounced off the sky-high ceilings, around the separating wall, and into the gourmet kitchen that doubled as a temporary study space for Shelby Wallingford, resident dog-sitter and daughter of Richard's friend from the office.

"Hi, Ms. Pike," Shelby answered. She closed her anatomy textbook and marked her place with a photo of her handsome boyfriend. "How was your day?"

"Not too bad, but it's not over yet," she said. "Shelby, do you happen to have any extra time next week?"

"I think so. Do you know how much time you'll need?"

"I'm not sure yet, but I'll know by tomorrow."

"Okay, Ms. Pike, just give me a call this weekend and let me know. I'll work it out for you."

"I would really appreciate that. I know its last minute, but I wouldn't spring this on you if it weren't important. Here, let me pay you in advance. That way it's covered if I don't see you before...I don't even know what. Anyway, just in case."

Madison reached into her black leather briefcase and pulled out three crisp one-hundred-dollar bills. "Shelby, you're a lifesaver."

"Thanks, Ms. Pike. You don't have to do that." She stared at the bills with wide eyes.

"Please. You deserve it. When you become a famous doctor, you might remember me," she answered with a chuckle as she put her wallet back into her briefcase.

Shelby packed up her knapsack of study materials and grabbed her giant purple umbrella to shield her from the pelting rain that promised to drench her with her first step outside.

"Can I call you a cab? It's really bad out there." Madison worried about Shelby's trek home. She didn't live far, but her hundred-pound frame was no match for this storm's punch.

"No, thank you. I'm going to tough it out. I kinda like the thrill of walking in bad storms. The daredevil in me, I guess." She shrugged her shoulders and leaned down to kiss Judge and Jury, who did not want to see her leave.

"Okay, but seriously. Be extra careful."

"Will do, Ms. Pike. Thanks again."

Madison shed her drenched attire on her way to her bedroom decorated in part by Alicia Carter, designer extraordinaire, confidant, and best friend. Alicia's award-winning designs filled every room, but Maddie's influence dominated the bedroom. Her wildest addition to her lair was in the form of a black leather swing suspended in midair that required Richard to do all the work. The harness was just high enough for him to move her perfect, naked body back and forth just the way she liked it. Every stroke, every thrust, hit it right every time. As far as Richard was concerned, the bedroom is where she did her best work.

Madison pressed the remote electric button on the right of the nightstand to draw the blackout shades. The murky skyline disappeared behind the fabric one inch at a time.

She stood in front of the mirror and thought of the naive teenage girl she once was. The successful woman she'd become didn't erase her pain or fill her soul in the way she had hoped. Despite the personal tragedy she'd endured so many years ago, she'd made it. But not unscathed. No one would ever know the confident, beautiful woman who stared back at her in the mirror was an empty shell who carried a guilt that tainted every part of her life. Her twin sister Michelle would never approve of her emotional cage or blame her for what happened that afternoon in Timberton Park.

Maddie leaned over and opened the wooden chest. She pulled out a letter she'd written to Michelle just days after her disappearance and read it aloud.

"I'm so sorry. If only... If only I'd let you be. I'm sorry for always thinking my ideas were better than yours. I'm sorry I always made you feel like you had to do what I said. If I hadn't coaxed you into coming to the park with me, Jordan, and Brandon that Saturday afternoon instead of going to work with Mom and Dad at the market like you always did, you'd still be here with us. You were sad that day. I didn't know why and I didn't take the time to ask you. I only meant to cheer you up. You said you didn't want to go. But I thought I knew better. I'm so sorry. Please come home. I love you. Signed, Maddie."

She folded the letter up into four squares and placed it back in the wooden box among other trinkets that belonged to Michelle. Her need to talk to her sister didn't stop with the last sentence.

"Mom and Dad worked their tails off to give us a better life. And I took away your chance to live yours. I'm so sorry." She focused on the mirror with a blank stare. For a moment, she felt a sense of peace come over her like never before. Unsure of what to make of it, she finished her apology. "Pike's market grew into Timberton's go-to grocery store. Remember how Dad used to tell customers that smiles, friendship, and laughter were free of charge. You used to love his silly slogans. I miss you."

Ally called right on cue for their customary evening chat. "Hey, girl. Just checking in with you. How goes it?

"Hey. Good timing." Her voice cracked in three places.

"Okay, what's wrong? I can read you like a book. Spill."

"I'm just standing here ruminating about the past and you know how that goes. One thing leads to another." Her sentence finished with a deep sigh.

"Uh oh. That's a slippery slope." Ally interrupted her with the intent to discourage that train ride, but Maddie kept going down the track.

"I was just thinking of Old Mrs. Proctor. Did I ever tell you about her?"

"No, I don't think so."

"She was a little old woman who came into Pike's Market every morning between 9:00 a.m. and 12:00 noon. She hobbled over to the café and staked claim to a table right in the middle of the foot traffic on purpose. 'A little coffee, a little TV, and you, my dear sweet girl who sits before me now. It's what I live for," she would say to Michelle, who sat with her every Saturday and listened to her stories.

"Aww, that's super sweet. She sounds like a nice lady."

"She passed away a year before Michelle went missing. The whole town attended the funeral," Maddie said, sorry she hadn't given the old woman any of her time. "Old Mrs. Proctor wasn't a rich woman, but her husband left her a good amount of money when he passed. A few hundred thousand dollars or so. She left that money to all the friends she made at the café, a big portion allotted to Michelle."

"Wow! That's kinda amazing, but that can't be what has you in a mood. What else?"

A few seconds of silence followed. Ally pressed harder. "Come on, what's got your panties in a bunch?"

"I got a message from Detective Hanoy today."

Ally was the only person who knew the whole story. The truth and nothing but the truth.

"There it is. That's it. I knew there had to be something else." She squealed and slapped her knee at the same time, proud that she knew her better than anyone else on the planet did. "Have you talked with him yet?"

"Not yet. I'm more than a little nervous about it."

"You'll be fine. You always are. You handle the toughest of the tough every day. You can handle this. Call me when you can. Let me know what's up."

"Okay, will do. Thanks for always being there."

"Of course. Always. Love you, girl."

"Love you back." Maddie hung up the phone.

Exposed inside and out, more vulnerable than she was comfortable with, she held her half of a unity pendant in the palm of her hand, the pendant her parents had given the girls on their seventh birthday. Their mom said it was a special gift to remind them they were stronger when they came together as one. Maddie still wore it each day and only removed it from her neck when the guilt choked her.

She put it on the nightstand and returned to her place in front of the mirror to complete what developed into an afternoon of self-examination. Her hand travelled down to her flat stomach, then to each side of her hips. Her physical form was void of imperfections by most people's standards, but the flaws she carried within ran deep underneath the surface of her skin. Her peers admired the career she built, the life she had, and the men she dated. She seemed to have the perfect life. For the first time she felt like an imposter in her own body, like she had fooled everyone, even herself.

Richard would be home soon. A shower and a glass of wine seemed like a good way to kill time. Just as Maddie headed to the spa-like shower big enough to hold five people, a ringtone reminiscent of the 1970s blared from her cell phone's tiny speaker.

"Hello, Madison Pike here."

"Madison, Hello. This is Detective Hanoy from the Timberton Lake, Louisiana Police Department."

"Yes, hello, Detective." She knew this old-timer well, as did all townies in Timberton. The pins and needles sharpened in her belly. She made small talk long enough to calm herself down. "Dad told me you and Penelope became grandparents this year. Congratulations are in order."

"Yes, we did. Thank you. Our daughter Ann had beautiful twin girls Ella and Elizabeth."

"Twins?" She felt jealous of the newborn baby twins, a shameful and ridiculous notion she could not stop. "You'll be a wonderful grandfather."

"I still see your mom and dad every week at the grocery store. They are doing a great job with the place. I don't know what our town would do without Pike's Market," Roger said in his low, authoritative voice. "We've been relying on them for the best fixings in town for the past forty years."

Maddie knew their casual banter had reached its end and the real purpose of his call was on deck.

With a gentle delivery, Roger gave her the news. "Maddie, this is hard for me to report, but I'm just gonna come right out and say it, Okay? Your sister's body has been found."

Maddie froze. Silent and in shock, she dropped to the plush carpet, her naked body cushioned by the threads.

"There was a fire some months ago at the construction site at the Old Timber Yard by the lake. The site was destroyed. Kingston Enterprises purchased the land in order to expand the park."

"Kingston Enterprises?" Tears muffled her words.

"Yes, Jordan's father's company. You remember it right?"

"Yes, of course."

"Well, a crew was clearing the area to begin building. They found her body buried several feet below the surface wrapped in a blanket, fully clothed, wearing a man's sweatshirt. Her head was placed on a pillow. It was like someone was trying to keep her comfortable."

"I can't believe it," she said with her eyes fixed on a wall sconce. Her anger and sadness mixed together like a toxic cocktail and caused her eyes to turn from blue to red; blood vessels swelled from the acid in her tears.

"There is someone here with me at the station right now who insisted on being in on this call."

"Okay?" she said, unsure of who it could be.

After a brief moment of silence, a familiar voice joined the conversation.

"Maddie, it's Jordan."

"Jordan?" she answered with a dose of unexpected adrenaline "So good to hear your voice. I can't believe all this." Her forehead landed in her hand as she rose from the floor.

"I'm here with Detective Hanoy. I insisted on being here when he called you."

"Jordan? Is he sure?"

"Yes. I'm afraid so."

"Do Mom, Dad, and Brandon know yet?" she said.

"Given the circumstances, we thought we should call you first. I'll see Brandon later at the ranch and fill him in. We'll have to tell them soon. The press is all over it."

"We searched for years. The entire town searched for years. No one could find her. It has been nearly nine years and now..." Her voice disappeared mid-sentence.

"I know, Maddie. This isn't the closure anyone wanted. You'll get through this—*we'll* get through this. I'll be by your side every step of the way if you want me to be," he said in an effort to console her.

"Maddie, this is Detective Hanoy again. I have to ask you to come to back Timberton as soon as possible."

Silence was her only reaction.

After the dead air choked her to near unconsciousness, she found her voice. "Yes, I should come. I should be with my family. It won't be easy to see Mom."

"I'll go with you," Jordan said. Given the context of their breakup, he did not expect his offer to be well received, but he wouldn't take no for an answer.

"I'm not sure."

"You're not in any condition to make decisions right now. Let's talk tomorrow and discuss details." Jordan's kind heart had not hardened from life's tragedies.

"Goodnight, Maddie," the detective said. "I'm sorry to contact you with this upsetting news."

"Thank you for your call. And Jordan, thank you for being there."

"You will always be my girl."

Jordan's final six words sent a chill down her back to the tip of her toes. She hadn't spoken to him since she'd left Timberton, but kept tabs on him through her brother Brandon, who volunteered at Kingston Ranch on weekends in between his duties as Timberton's most decorated firefighter.

The sound of Jordan's voice cracked her armor. He climbed up from the hidden chambers of her heart and pulled at the strings. The delicate, imaginary force field she spun to keep her nightmares locked up and her love for him at a safe distance collapsed the moment he cast his spell.

"You'll always be my girl." Did he really just say that? The very same promise he'd made to me day after day so many years ago? Can I believe him? I want to believe him.

Unable to hang up, she listened to nothing but air until the line went dead. Her world morphed into slow motion. She sat on the side of her bed, in the dark for what seemed like an eternity.

Richard will be home soon, she thought with no real plan on how to break this news. *I have to come clean. How will I tell him the truth now? He doesn't even know I had a twin. And Jordan?*

In a zombie-like state, she made her way into the shower. Scalding hot water beat down on her soft skin like pellets from a BB gun. Her flesh turned fiery red from the heat, but she felt no pain. Her numb exterior met the inner turbulence that brewed inside her and froze her pain amidst the hot steam, a form of self-defense she used more than once to prepare herself for Richard's persecution whenever he felt threatened. In his mind, when it came to Jordan, she was guilty until proven innocent.

CHAPTER TWO

As Maddie exited her temporary cell with near first-degree burns, she heard Richard's baritone voice in the living room. The content of his words made no difference. His mere arrival stung her like swarm of hornets.

Another man joined in the chatter. She didn't recognize the second voice, but didn't balk at the gift of more time.

Maddie dried her locks and fixed a tight bun on top of her head. The light fabric of the short, sexy, red robe Richard gave her for Christmas last year soothed her burnt flesh. Just as she peeked around the corner to identify the mystery male, Richard barreled into her chest on his way into the bedroom to find her.

"Whoa, there, babe." He grabbed her waist to steady her.

She straightened and her eyes locked with his.

"You look absolutely stunning," Richard said, drawn to her exposed cleavage, her robe too small to cover her treats.

He outlined her face with his finger, then cupped her chin in the palm of his hands. Her mouth relaxed as she let him land a soft, tender kiss on her parted lips. Her mediocre response sent a clear message.

She dropped her chin and nestled her head into his hard-earned pecs, his white dress shirt already unbuttoned to his waist.

"What's wrong, sexy lady? Tell me." He lifted her head to come in for another kiss.

She shrugged and deflected his second attempt. "Who's out there, Richard?"

"It's Pete Wallingford. Why? Does it matter?"

"No, it's just that I have to talk to you. It's important. Can you ask him to come back another time? Please?"

"Come on. It's Friday night. It can't be more important than that," he said in jest, but her mood did not allow her to be amused. Under any other circumstance, her playful side would meet his and he'd end up inside her, but tonight he set her off in a different way.

Annoyed by Richard's immediate dismissal of her request and the fact that she'd beat him up in her thoughts before he even walked through the door, Richard had no chance for mercy.

"Fine. Have it your way. As usual," she answered with a sharp tongue, a characteristic she was not proud of and only revealed in the courtroom when necessary. Maddie sashayed out into the living room in her provocative attire with the intent of poking the bear and pissing him off.

"What's got you so bitchy tonight?"

Maddie looked straight ahead and made her way to the kitchen. She reached for a wine glass from the top shelf, her round, tight assets on display for all to see.

"Hey, Pete. How are you?" she said as if she didn't have a care in the world. "You missed Shelby. She was here today. Great girl you have there. She will be a big success someday."

Pete's mouth wiped the floor and his eyes popped beyond their sockets. Her robe covered just enough to rob Pete of the best day of his life.

"Uh, yeah." Pete cleared his throat and pulled up his trousers with both hands in an effort to adjust himself without being obvious. "Hi, uh, Madison.

You look...I mean you are...uh...what I mean to say is, haven't seen you around the office in a while."

Pete looked to the floor, afraid to stare too long. His opportunities to come this close to a girl like Maddie in the state she was in were slim to none. He rubbed his forehead with his left hand like he was just hit with a baseball bat.

Richard didn't miss a beat. Amused by it all, his ego filled up like air pumped into a tire. His head inflated to maximum pounds per square inch. In her perturbed state, she neglected to consider that Richard loved to show her off, dressed or not.

After a couple of drinks, an hour of flirtatious banter, and frequent trips to the bathroom, Pete headed home for the night with an unexpected satisfaction.

"Funny guy, that Pete," she said as she played with the empty carafe of cabernet. "I'm glad he stayed." The four glasses she'd downed had given her a sufficient buzz to take the edge off.

"Well, I'm glad he left." Richard came up behind her, aroused by her banter with Pete. He removed the silver clip from the bun that held her wet hair on top of her head. The long strands fell to meet the tousled tresses that framed her face. He pushed himself closer. Her sweet scent covered him, his face buried in her.

"Richard." His advances proved too easy to accept.

He spun her around and slipped off her robe, removed only by his talented tongue. He dropped to his knees, spread apart her long legs with no resistance, and licked her where she liked it most.

"No. I can't." She grabbed his face and pulled him back up, the mood broken with no warning.

"Damn it, Madison." He backed off in complete frustration. "What! What is it?"

"Stop. Just stop."

Richard and Madison sat separately in silence for a half hour or so to cool off before they said words they would both regret. Finally, Maddie ended the standoff, took his right hand, and led him to the small, intimate loveseat Ally suggested she buy for that space.

"Wait here," she said and left the room for a moment.

Already frustrated, tired, and buzzed, he surrendered, resting his head on the back of the loveseat. She returned with a large, brown photo album trimmed in gold and one small, lima bean-shaped scrapbook.

Maddie sat with a calculated space between them. She held the large book on her lap and placed the lima bean on the coffee table in front of him for later. He formed an inward slope with his eyebrows that exposed his curiosity.

"Okay." Maddie took a deep breath and opened to the first page. "We've known each other for about five years."

"Yes, and we have a great life," he answered.

"I know. We do. Please. Just listen."

"Okay, fine. Get to the point, please." His patience dwindled.

She looked down at the album. "There are just some things you don't know about me, things about my past that I didn't share with you for my own selfish reasons."

Richard hated surprises. She hoped he would hear all the facts before he convicted her in his mind. Even his clients received that courtesy.

"Innocent until proven guilty," she said to remind him of a basic premise in their profession. He did not appreciate the ethics lesson and instead met her schooling with a judgmental stare. She wanted this exchange to end, so she pushed her way through just to get it over with.

"You know a little about Mom, Dad, and my brother Brandon, but you don't know why I left my family and a life I once loved."

"Yeah, we've talked plenty about that," he said with a skillful shift in subject matter. "Let's go to bed now." He leaned her backward, pinned her hands above her head and hovered over her exposed nipples.

"Richard, I'm serious here. You have to hear me out."

After an eye roll and a short pause, he let her up and feigned interest. "Okay, okay. Go on."

"I left Timberton to go to college in New York... to run from something. I thought that if I immersed myself in a new life far enough away from home, I could forget. Move on. Be free of guilt."

"Maddie, what are we talking about here?"

"Look at these photos. Mom, Dad, me, Brandon." She waved her finger over a few pictures on the page in an effort to speed things up. "And here you can see Pike's Market, Timberton Park, and Timberton Lake."

"Yes, okay."

"Well, this photo here." She poked it with her finger. "This is The Old Timber Yard where all the kids in town used to hang out, drink, and raise hell. We'd sneak in through a broken door that no one ever bothered to fix. It was a huge warehouse filled with cords of timber to be shipped out. It was more like a holding tank, not very well staffed. It was easy to get in and out without anyone noticing a thing."

"Must we continue?" Richard asked. "Let's fuck."

She closed the large photo album and bounced it off the table. He didn't want to know any more. He didn't care to know any more. All he wanted was to get her on the swing and watch her scream.

Maddie picked up the small photo album, shook it in his face, and forced him to pay attention whether he wanted to or not.

"This is what you don't know, you selfish, horny bastard." At this point, she wasn't one bit concerned about his temper, but was thankful she hadn't yet seen signs of it. "Now look at these photos. What do you see?"

Richard took the album from her hand and glanced at it to appease her. The sooner he moved her along, the sooner he could get her into bed. Not quite sure what he saw, he was compelled to take a second look.

"What?" His eyes focused in on two girls as he leaned over to take a closer look. "Who is this?" he pointed to the carbon copy standing next to Maddie. Two identical faces stared back at him.

"That is Michelle. My identical twin."

"Are you serious? Five years and you never mentioned her?"

"There is a certain part of my life I just couldn't relive. I buried it. It was a matter of survival. If I dragged it all up five years ago, it would've killed me. And as time went by, it was just easier to leave it alone."

"Bury what?"

Here goes. She repositioned herself on the two-person loveseat that seemed to shrink by the second. This exchange was suited more for the wraparound sofa that allowed for more space between them in case he went ballistic when she mentioned Jordan's name. "Michelle went missing. We were 19 years old at the time."

"What?"

"Jordan, Brandon, Michelle, and I were all at Timberton Park on a Saturday afternoon in July. There was a fair in the park that day and I talked Michelle into coming with us instead of helping my parents at the market like she did every Saturday. If it wasn't for me, she wouldn't have been there that day. Next thing we know, she's gone. Nowhere to be found."

Richard stood up and raised his arms over his head in silence. The mere mention of Jordan's name caused him to spring off the sofa and walk around the room like a ping-pong ball slapped around by novice players.

"Say something, Richard."

"Go on," he said without even a glance her way.

"The whole town looked for her. A few leads, but nothing panned out. There were some people of interest, particularly one of her friends, Colin Stone. He was an odd kid in our class. Really quiet. Very strange. I don't remember him ever lifting his eyes off the floor when he walked through the hallways. I do remember he was bullied a lot in school despite his large size. Michelle always protected him. They became good friends, which I didn't like. I always discouraged that relationship."

"The police never found anything on him?" he asked as he stared out the window.

"Nothing. You would've loved her, Richard," she said with an attempt to appeal to his human side. "She was the kindest soul you'd ever meet. Good to everyone. Happy all the time. She woke up early every Sunday morning to dress for church and never missed a week. Her faith was unshakable, and even at a young age she knew she wanted to devote her life to help those less fortunate." Maddie paused. Her sincere reflection felt like overdue permission to miss her.

An awkward moment of silence filled the air. He offered no comment following her heart-felt confession.

"Michelle saved me from my self-absorbed ways. I wasn't always kind to her. She deserved better."

"Well, you can be a bitch sometimes," Richard said with a tone that was as sharp as shards of glass.

She chose to ignore his comment rather than escalate it. "I feel guilty that I tried so hard to forget her." Maddie wept.

"Is that what tonight's important phone call was all about?"

"Yes. It was Detective Hanoy. He leads all criminal investigations in Timberton and surrounding areas. I consider him a friend."

"What did he want?"

"Her body was found yesterday." She blurted out the news.

"What?" he asked with the first sign of any real interest. "Where? How?"

"Detective Hanoy said that there was a fire at The Old Timber Yard. It was total teardown. Kingston Enterprises bought the land and began construction to expand Timberton Park. Jordan's father thought it would be a great way to give back to the community that has been so good to him."

"Jordan's father owns Kingston Enterprises?" Richard said with a measure of respect intended solely for Jordan's father. "Kingston Enterprises is a pretty big deal."

"Yes, Wesley Kingston is the owner and Jordan is the Director of Development."

"I thought Jordan was a handyman on their family's ranch. Raised cows or something like that."

"Not exactly, but what would be wrong with that?" she said, fed up with his air of superiority. "Jordan works for his father now as the Director of Development during the week and holds a camp at the ranch on the weekends to help disabled children learn how to ride. It helps them heal. Gives them hope and confidence."

"And how do you know all this? I thought you hadn't talked to Jordan since you came to New York."

"My brother Brandon works at the ranch." She left the second half of his question unanswered.

"He does? What else?" He waved his hand in the air. His voice deepened. "Is there anything else you want to tell me?"

"Yes, there's one more thing."

"Okay, let's have it."

"Detective Hanoy wants me get to down to Timberton as soon as possible."

"What!" Richard shook his head like a bull ready to stomp on its rider.

In an effort to defuse him, she said, "I'm not sure I can bring any value to his investigation at this point. And frankly, I'm not sure it's good for my family either. My mother blamed me for Michelle's disappearance and she still hasn't forgiven me for it."

Richard sat in silence. His anger turned his spray tan into a strange shade of red at the thought of her and Jordan thrown together again.

"My mother hasn't spoken to me since." Maddie elaborated on that thought and stayed away from the other lane. "I can tell she can hardly stand to talk to me. I remind her of Michelle so much. Our personalities were very different, but our mannerisms were so much alike."

"So what are you gonna do?" he asked, on his third shade of red. A virtual wedge worked its way between them.

"I really don't know. I'm too drained to think anymore." She rose from the loveseat, her robe disheveled. "I'm going to bed."

She extended the olive branch and held out her perfectly manicured hand for him to take. "Come to bed with me. We'll figure this out in the morning."

Her gesture met with a blank stare. Her hand hung in the air untouched.

Maddie's faithful pups jumped off the kitchen chairs where they'd sat through the entire exchange. Judge threatened Richard with a growl and followed Maddie into the bedroom while Jury wiggled by him with her fury nose in the air.

As much as she wanted to tell Richard he had no reason to be jealous or worried, she couldn't. Guilty as charged.

CHAPTER THREE

Maddie lay awake and restless, alone in their king-size bed. Richard had passed out on the sofa in full business attire. The pressure to make the right choice squeezed her heart tighter with each minute that went by. "Stay or go?" she ruminated throughout the night.

The Saturday morning daylight hours arrived. Maddie's lack of shuteye didn't stop her from a 4:00 a.m. pot of coffee to satisfy her with a much-needed dose of caffeine. A rich aroma of Italian coffee drifted across the living room, carried by a cool breeze that entered through a small space beneath the window Richard cracked open last night.

Her first task of the day was to call her best friend. Maddie was certain Ally wouldn't mind the hour. Chances are she hadn't even gone to bed yet. Friday nights with her brilliant, right-brained friends from The Art Extravaganza, an organization she built from the ground up that gave new artists a platform to show their work, turned into the likes of an erotic film. Late night cell phone pictures of an intoxicated, scantily clad Alicia simulating sex acts with expensive sculptures appeared on Maddie's phone many Saturday mornings.

As Maddie dialed from the den for privacy, she heard movement.

"Damn it," she said to herself as she hung up just as the call connected. She hurried to the kitchen so Richard wouldn't accuse her of sneaking a call to Jordan, an act she'd been falsely accused of too many times over the years.

Richard went straight into the bathroom to clean up. Five minutes later, he emerged bare-naked. All his glory hung out, as impressive as always.

"Morning," Richard said as he walked past her into the kitchen.

"Morning." she said, unable to get a read on him.

He used his long reach to remove two coffee cups from the top shelf of the new designer cabinets in their state of the art kitchen. His broad, muscular back fanned out like a cobra ready to strike. Maddie found herself lost in each muscle that seemed to flex on its own.

He turned and walked toward her. The space closed between them. His manhood landed first.

"Are we okay?" He slid his hands under her robe and across her soft breasts. "Do you know how delicious you smell? What you do to me?" His mouth grazed the tip of her ear. "I'm not afraid of much. But I am afraid of losing you."

She wanted him to please her and run wild in the sexual playground of their bedroom like they did every Saturday morning, but the thought of Jordan consumed her. His voice replayed in her mind like a broken record. *You'll always be my girl.*

Before another word was spoken, Maddie's phone rang; caller ID showed Ally's name.

"Don't answer that," Richard said.

Maddie never did take orders from Richard and this time was no exception.

"Hey, Ally."

"Good morning, early bird," she said, half asleep. "I saw you called. You okay?"

"Not really."

"Why? What's the matter?" Ally said and just as fast added, "Hold on. Let me throw on a t-shirt or something and go into my design room."

"Why? Do you have company? Someone named Olivio, by any chance?" Maddie asked, taunting her about her boss.

"Yes, I know. I said I wasn't going to go there, but I couldn't help myself. After the art show, we went out for some drinks and, well, he's just hot. What can I say?"

"Dangerous territory, my friend." Maddie reminded her of the disastrous outcome the last time she ventured down that road.

"Yes, so right," Ally said, unable to disagree with her friend's assessment of her foibles. "But the sex rattles my brain."

"You said that about your last boss too. And remember how well that worked out for you?"

"Yes, so right again, but enough about me. Tell me. What's going on?"

"Can I call you back in a bit?"

"I'm here when you need me."

"Sounds good. Catch up in a little while."

Maddie rose from the bar stool and walked to the bathroom without so much as a look in Richard's direction. In haste, she left her cell phone on the kitchen counter.

Richard hung over the breakfast bar in a thoughtful pose. With each sip of coffee, he contemplated his next move. He knew he would have to fight to make her stay even if she wasn't ready to admit it.

He took three steps from the kitchen when two consecutive text messages came through on Maddie's phone that lay face up right where she'd left it.

His strong arms extended straight out in front of him, the machine squarely between his hands as his head dropped in frustration. Richard read only the first couple lines of the messages, the first few words displayed on the screen. "*It was great to hear your voice yesterday. I'm...*" the text ended. "*I miss you.*" read the text that followed.

"Maddie," he called to her as he walked toward the bathroom door. "Can I talk to you for a minute please?"

"Sure. Just a sec." She took her time and stalled as long as she could.

More than a minute went by, and with each second, Richard became more jealous and angry that she'd left out her communication with Jordan in her explanation of the latest events. A fact he considered relevant under the circumstances.

As soon as the door opened, he came at her like she was the world's most notorious criminal.

"Tell me more about Jordan."

"What?" She sat on the bed.

"When did you speak to him last?"

"I don't know. It's been a long time."

"Are you sure about that?" Enraged by her lie, he puffed out his chest.

She just stared at him with no response.

"Well?"

Her blank stare continued. For the first time, she was afraid to speak. Afraid of Richard.

His temper escalated to new levels. He leaned over her, his face inches from hers. "Why are you lying to me?"

Petrified of the man before her, she continued her act. "What are you talking about?"

He grabbed her neck with his right hand. His grip tightened while his left hand raised high above her. A closed fist came at her terrified face and stopped an inch away from her delicate jawline. Before a knockout punch landed, he stopped. "I'm so sorry." He threw his hands in the air in full surrender.

"You bastard!" She slapped him across the face as hard as she could, a mark left on him that would last a lifetime.

He had made her decision too easy. There was nothing more to think over. She packed a bag, gathered her belongings, and headed to the airport to catch the next flight to Louisiana.

The rain and wind continued from yesterday, but she was oblivious to it. She arrived at the airport as fast as the cab could get her there.

She hadn't yet looked at her cell phone. It had landed at the bottom of her purse with all the other small items she grabbed on her way out the door.

When she pulled it out to call Ally, it all became clear. The texts said it all.

Maddie called and left a message. "Ally, you are not going to believe what just happened. Anyway, I'm on my way to the airport and heading home to Timberton. I'll fill you in on everything when I get there. I don't know how long I'll be gone. Not really sure about anything right now. Talk to you later."

Maddie jumped on the next available flight and arrived in Louisiana that evening. Desperate for a chance to breathe and slow things down a bit, she checked into a hotel just outside of town without notifying anyone of her arrival.

The next morning brought an eighty-degree day. Above average for the month of January in the Timberton area this year. Maddie's first move was to head to Kingston Ranch. The timing was perfect. She knew Brandon and Jordan held their riding camp for disabled and terminally ill children every Sunday, an event she wished she could see ever since Brandon told her about it so many years ago.

Maddie walked through the hotel lobby. She earned the attention of every man, and woman, in sight. Her long, tan, sexy legs never ended and her fit rear peeked through the bottom of her shorts in a tasteful way. No one could look away. No one wanted to.

Her hair flowed down her back, and she oozed sex appeal. The young man at the front desk didn't move a muscle. Except for one. As she walked out the front door, his eyes followed her until every part of her cleared the corner of the building.

"Whoa, did you see her?" the desk clerk gasped.

His female coworker flashed him a jealous smile and said, "Keep it down, big boy." She had some knowledge of his physical attributes.

Madison sped out of the parking lot, the top down on her luxury rental car. With a ponytail tied tightly behind her neck to combat the wind that would otherwise generate a feast of tangled strands, she headed to Kingston Ranch, only a few miles away.

What am I going to say to him? Butterflies invaded her belly like she was sixteen years old again.

The ranch never failed to impress. Two hundred acres of green fields and tall timber as far as the eye could see. Beautiful, majestic horses grazed in the green pastures and stallions galloped, graceful and proud. So much life. So much peace in the air. She was drawn right back in.

Madison entered the front gate that remained open during camp hours and continued the drive up the dirt road. She parked near the stables, then walked toward the arena on the other side of the horse corrals.

With every step, she regretted her decision to leave Timberton. The thrill of the city and the kind of life she worked so hard for paled in comparison to the appreciation for life she felt as soon as she stepped onto the ranch.

Once she reached the arena, the warmth of the day caused her to perspire more than her hot yoga class. Her tank top hugged her, exposing her excitement. Going braless made her feel sexy and free, a sharp contrast from the routine of her rigid city life.

Madison approached the door to the arena when she heard, "Maddie?"

Brandon strutted over, his strong, lean physique looking healthy. With no effort, he picked her up and twirled her around as if she weighed nothing at all. "What? You're here?"

"Hey you," she said, overjoyed to see her brother again. "It's been far too long, little brother." Without going into any detail as to what finalized her decision to come, she gave him a hug worthy of a world record.

"How are you? By now I'm sure you know more about the latest developments than I do," she said, her arm still wrapped around his broad shoulders as they walked.

"Yes, and I'm upset. Damn mad all over again."

"I know, Brandon. I'm so sorry."

"It's all over the news. Hard to hear. Very hard to hear." He hung his head.

"What about Mom and Dad?"

"They aren't ready for this at all."

"Yeah, I figured. What do they know so far?"

"They only know Michelle was found in the Old Timber Yard and an investigation is under way. Mom has secluded herself in the house. She won't come out. And Dad is going to the work at the market every day like nothing has changed. It's a mess."

Maddie grabbed her head in silence and paused for a moment. "Brandon, did I do the right thing by coming here? Is my presence going to make it worse for them?"

"I think you were right to come. Dad will want to see you for sure. Mom? I think it will take her more time."

"I know they still blame me. Dad tries not to show it, but I can tell he has a hard time looking at me, just like Mom does. Maybe I shouldn't let them know I'm even here. I don't know what good I can do anyway."

"No. Stay. Talk to Detective Hanoy and get the details. You will want to know. It will be hard at first, but it's the right thing."

"Okay, I'll talk to him. But then we'll see."

"We'll give him a call together when you're ready. Why don't you go see Jordan first? He was hoping you'd come. He's champing at the bit to see you again," Brandon added with a chuckle.

"Okay. Wait. Tell me about you. I want to hear about you first." Before he could answer, she added, "You look great. Really great."

"Thanks, Sis. You don't look so bad yourself." Brandon put his arm around her and guided her toward the arena door.

Her heart ached whenever she felt like her decision to leave Timberton might have let Brandon down in some way. This moment was no exception.

"How's work going?" Her smile widened.

"Good, Sis. Love my job. We have some new firefighters coming aboard soon. And one is a young lady. Blew all the guys away in the training exercises."

"Really? I like to hear that. Things have come a long way since I left town, huh?"

"Yeah, that's true. Chances are good I'll be promoted to captain. I would be the youngest fire chief Timberton has ever seen," he said. His torso straightened.

"Good stuff, Brandon. I'm so proud of you. Timberton is lucky to have you at the helm. Strong, reliable, handsome devil like you," she said with a light punch square into his six-pack abs. It looked more like an eight-pack these days.

"Yeah, the ladies seem to like it," Brandon answered with his signature coy smile known to drop the pants off most girls with no real effort.

"There's that smile," Maddie winked. "I see you still got it."

Before she could say another word, Brandon opened the arena door and good thing he was there to do it. Its giant size needed every bit of Brandon's six-foot-seven frame to move it.

There stood Jordan. In full view. More impressive and handsome than she ever remembered. Her face softened at the sight of him and her admiration was immeasurable.

Behind him, the lines of beautiful children with various disabilities waited with remarkable patience for their turn to ride the majestic, grayish-white Arabian horses Jordan bred and raised. The arena was filled with trainers, teachers, staff, and medics who worked in unison to give the children a special experience. She'd forgotten what happiness and joy looked like. Nothing she accomplished matched the smiles he brought to the faces of the children.

Maddie moved closer, but stayed out of his line of sight. She was in awe of him.

"C'mon, Isabelle, sweetheart, let's get you up on White Shadow. It's your turn," Jordan said to the seven-year-old little girl next in line suffering from a rare bone disease.

Her arms reached out to him. Her eyes lit up brighter than any star. "Thanks, Mr. Jordan. I love White Shadow. She's my favorite horse."

"Well, I'm glad to hear it. Anything for you, miss," he said with a tip of his hat. After he made sure little Isabelle was saddled up and secure, one of his handlers jumped up and rode with her to make sure she'd be safe, her bones too weak to leave her on her own. Jordan led the horse around the arena by the harness with great care. Isabelle laughed with each careful step of the horse. It was as if White Shadow knew his purpose.

Madison watched Jordan until camp was over, then followed him to the stables where the horses were groomed.

"Jordan?" she said as she peeked around the stall where White Shadow boarded.

He turned his broad shoulders toward the familiar voice. In disbelief of the beauty who stared back at him, he tipped his cowboy hat backward to make sure his eyes hadn't played a trick on him. "Maddie?" he squinted. "Is that really you?"

He dropped everything in his grip, picked her up, and swung her around in circles just like he had when they were kids. It required no effort to lift her slender physique. His jaw-dropping build could lift a tractor and he could still carry on a conversation at the same time.

The spark between them could have ignited all the hay in the barn. He put her down one inch at the time. Every curve of her body passed through his hands and his seductive, light brown eyes sent her a clear message.

She felt him stiffen on the journey down his magnificent body. With a gentle push backward, she regained her composure before she lost all control.

"Wow, that's some greeting," she said. "I wasn't sure how you would react to seeing me."

He grabbed both her hands and took a step closer. Her palms sweated, her insides twisted, and her brain scrambled from his musk, a mix of hard work and fresh air. She never thought she'd be this close to him again.

"Maddie, I just want you to know that no matter what happened between us in the past, you will always be a part of me and I will always be happy to see you. I'm just sorry it's under these difficult circumstances," he said, sincere and saddened. "I am truly sorry about Michelle. I know how difficult it is to find out she is gone, and the way she... well, I'm just so sorry."

"Thank you, Jordan." Her effort to play it cool failed. Her hands trembled and exposed her desire to know him again. In a feeble attempt to hide the obvious, she changed the conversation. "This is all devastating to me. I'll call Detective Hanoy as soon as I leave here, and hopefully he can meet with me this evening. He doesn't even know I'm in town yet."

"He doesn't?" Jordan looked confused. "Isn't he the first person you'd want to see under these circumstances?"

She wanted to say, *No. All I've been thinking about is you since we spoke on the phone the other day.* But she didn't let on that her obsession with him returned the moment she heard his voice. Instead, she gave the answer she thought he expected. "Yes, of course. But I wanted to touch base with Brandon first. I knew I could find him here today."

"Ah. I thought maybe you just wanted to see... me."

She raised her head and looked at him, thinking he must have felt her heart beat outside her chest when he lifted her to the sky.

"Well, you'll never know for sure, will you?" She flirted right back. "What you did out there today. With the children. It was beautiful."

"Why don't you come back next weekend and meet them? They're amazing." He leaned down to pick up a rope on the bale of hay near the stall.

"I'm not sure I'll be here next weekend."

Jordan stood and gave her a look that would rattle most people. "What do you mean, you might not be here next weekend? It seems to me you have some things to take care of here in town, young lady." He threw the rope over the stall door. His ass looked too good in his denim jeans and his frame made his white t-shirt sing.

"We'll see," she said.

As he moved closer to her, his defenses, already impaired by her presence, diminished. Her mouth. Her eyes. The way she bit her lip. The attraction between them was raw and real. He found himself defenseless to stop it.

Jordan placed his hand at the nape just underneath her hair. He tugged on it with a gentle pull that tilted her head back the way he used to do when they were young. His lips hovered close to hers. His warm breath melted her like marshmallows over a fire.

"Mmm. As much as I want to…" He caressed her and drew her in further.

"Don't stop," she said with a heavy sigh. "How did I ever resist you?"

He paused and gave another seductive tug. The only thought that crossed his mind was how much he wanted to please her and show her how much he wanted to her. Needed her. Missed her.

He pressed his body against her. His erection, kept at bay only by his blue jeans, begged to escape. Her full lips parted with the tease of his wet tongue.

His hand ran around her tiny waist and rested on her perfect ass.

As Jordan laid her down in the hay to finish what he started, a voice echoed through the air that cut their connection like a razor-sharp knife.

"Jordan? Are you in here?"

"Down in the back!" He broke his hold on Maddie like she was contagious.

"Sorry to interrupt your meeting," the blonde-haired woman said. Her suspicious eyes looked Maddie up and down with daggers. "Are you here for one of the horses?"

"Ah, maybe. I'm here looking for something, that's for sure," Maddie said. She picked up on the pretentious and jealous vibe.

Jordan jumped in before their banter went to hell. "Madison Pike, I'd like you to meet Eliza West."

"Do you clean the stables here on the ranch?" Maddie asked.

"No," Eliza said. Her unsettled tone gave Maddie some satisfaction. "I'm Jordan's fiancée."

Blindsided by the news and unsure why Brandon hadn't thought to mention it in any one of their many conversations over the years, Maddie retained her composure and appeared unaffected. Without any desire to look at either one of them any longer, Maddie shook Jordan's hand and thanked him for the information. "I'll be in touch if I have any need for what you're selling."

She fought the urge to kick him in his softened crotch and walked away. Fit to be tied like cattle in a rodeo, she made her way across the arena, jumped in her convertible, and sped off.

"Damn it," Maddie's right hand bounced off the steering wheel more than once.

Eliza stared at Jordan in silence. The knot in her gut tightened with each second, waiting for him to come up with some kind of fabricated explanation she wouldn't believe. No matter what Jordan said to her from that moment on, she knew that girl had changed everything. Life as she knew it was over unless she did something about it.

Jordan grabbed the barn's push broom and swept the dry hay from the walkway of the barn to give Eliza a chance to cool off the molten lava that brewed just beneath her surface.

"Jordan, who was that?" Eliza grabbed the long stick out of his hand.

"Just and old friend." His composure stayed intact.

"Just an old friend, huh?"

"Yes, just an old friend."

Aware she was not going to get any more information on this girl from him, she put her anger aside and resumed her original mission to bring the focus back to her.

"Well, I came out here to tell you I made several appointments for us to go visit my top three wedding venues."

Jordan paused and stretched his neck so far to the left that it crackled in three places.

"Okay. When is it?"

"I booked us for the next three Sundays."

"No. You know I have the kids' camp on Sundays." He slapped both hands against the stable door.

"Oh, c'mon. You can skip it. Brandon will take over for you."

"You are some piece of work, Eliza." He shook his head as he grabbed the broom out of her hands, stared into her icy eyes, and pushed the hay without a word.

"Jordan?" Her persistence angered him even more.

"No chance. Change the appointments and that's the end of this conversation," he said with not so much as a glance her way.

Incensed at Jordan for reasons she had no right to, Maddie's blue eyes morphed into an opaque, jealous green as she drove with no destination in mind. Thanks to Timberton's small-town composition, Peg's Diner appeared within minutes.

Thrown off kilter from her encounter with Eliza, Maddie pulled into the diner parking lot, opened the car door, and slammed it hard enough to break the glass. "Damn it." She continued her jealous fit. The crack in the glass travelled farther up the window, but she was too enraged to care. Eliza's long locks and sexy legs went on for days. The competition had begun. One she planned to win.

As she walked toward the entrance, she paused and stared at the all too familiar establishment. Memories of the days of old circled her around in her mind like racecars on a racetrack. As strong and resilient as Maddie was, the last few hours had pushed her near her limit and challenged her resolve, what little she had left of it.

The local hangout hadn't changed a bit in all these years. It had been a landmark in Timberton for generations. The long, silver bullet-style diner displayed the same comfortable, interior Maddie remembered. Not a piece of memorabilia out of place. Photos captured the celebrities who had passed through town and continued to entertain. The red booths stayed bright. The long, white laminate counters with red and silver swivel stools packed in teenagers from town on a Sunday afternoon. Vanilla milk shakes, sky-high burgers, and homemade apple pie were still the foods of choice. Not a minute went by that Maddie didn't wish she could turn back the clock and stop time.

Peg Paulsen, the owner, recognized her right away. She was a spry seventy-year-old woman who didn't look a day over sixty.

"Madison. Hello, my dear." Peg greeted her with a tight embrace. "So good to see you. It's been so long."

"Hello, Mrs. Paulsen. Very good to see you."

"Please sit down and relax a bit. I'll get you a cup of coffee and some pie."

"Thank you, I would like that."

"I'm so very sorry to hear about the news. It must be very difficult for you."

"Yes, very painful." Maddie looked around the diner for a quiet area. "Would you mind if I used your back office to call Detective Hanoy? I'd like him to meet me here if he can," she asked. The possibility that the back office might not exist anymore didn't cross her mind for a second.

"Yes, dear. Of course you can. That Roger is such nice man. Please tell him I said hello, will you?"

"Of course. I certainly will."

"When you're ready, just go on back." Peg pointed to the door in the back corner. "It's not much, but it'll be quiet."

"Wonderful. That's very kind of you. Thank you."

While Mrs. Paulsen prepared the coffee and homemade apple pie, Maddie stepped through the door and called the detective to see if he could swing down to the diner. He was surprised she was in town, but without hesitation agreed to meet her at the diner in half an hour.

Maddie sat in a booth that faced the entrance so she wouldn't miss his arrival. Just as she finished eating all the apples out of the pie with the crust left behind, the detective hobbled in.

Still a debonair but older man, he walked with a noticeable limp he had acquired after his battle with cancer. It had aged him, but Brandon said he was cancer free and back on the job full-time.

"Madison." He tipped his hat to her in old-school fashion.

"Hello, detective." She rose from her seat while he slid into the booth.

His leg lagged behind and banged into the table. The grimace on his face showed some of the pain that remained from his ordeal.

"Thank you for meeting me on such short notice."

"Please sit." He waved his hand, and signaled her not to bother to get up on his account. "I'm glad you came. Good to see you."

"I must tell you I am more than a little anxious to know the details."

"I won't beat around the bush here."

"Please. Yes, please just tell me. What happened?"

"As you know, Kingston Enterprises purchased the Old Timber Yard after a fire condemned it in order to excavate and expand Timberton Park."

"Yes."

"And you also know that while excavating the property, Michelle's body was found buried several feet below the surface wrapped in a blanket, fully clothed, wearing a man's sweatshirt, her head placed on a pillow as if someone was trying to keep her comfortable in her demise."

Maddie's head drooped with each word. "Please. Continue."

"What I haven't told you is that it appears that she was beaten badly, and from what we can tell, she was impaled on a sharp object, possibly a pipe, which entered through her back and exited through her chest wall."

"What?" She grabbed her head. "Beaten? Was she raped?"

"We don't think so."

"Who would do this? Why? This is just unbelievable." Maddie couldn't hold back tears.

"We don't have any leads yet, but you can be damn sure I am not going to give up until I find the sons of bitches who did this."

"Did you investigate everyone? Every lead? Maybe you missed something?" Her tone was harsh. Patrons on the far side of the diner looked to see what all the ruckus was about.

"We are talking to everyone again as we speak. The case was reopened. It's now a homicide investigation and we are working on it."

"You're not working fast enough." She hit the Formica tabletop with an open hand and knocked over the plastic ketchup bottle.

"I understand you are upset. We're doing everything we can."

"I'm sorry. I'm sure you are, but I just can't handle the fact that she suffered. Beaten and impaled on a sharp object? We have to find out who did this."

"It's tragic. Truly tragic. We will get him, them, whoever they are. Believe me, we will find the truth and when we do, they'll wish they were never born."

"What about that shady character, Colin Stone, who used to be obsessed with Michelle? Is he still around? I'll never forget him. I had a real problem with that kid."

"He does still live in town," the detective confirmed after a pause. "We've got him on our radar too. But ever since the news story broke, he's MIA."

No sooner did Roger finish his sentence than in walked Colin through the diner's front entrance.

Madison locked in on his empty eyes. His ragged, dirty clothes hid the athletic frame he still possessed, but guilt on his face gave him away.

Right on cue, he raced out the door, knocking over two regulars. His heavy foot missed the woman's head by inches.

"Wait!" Maddie's pitch would have cracked a crystal glass. She chased after him, but by the time she made it out to the parking lot, he was long gone.

"Damn it." Her hands rested on her knees. She took one last look past the edge of the lot, down the tree-lined road to see if she could get lucky enough to catch a glimpse of him. *I have to stay. For now.*

CHAPTER FOUR

The night hour closed in. Exhausted and drained, Maddie decided to head back to the hotel. Her sister's demise haunted her and the fact that Jordan was engaged added to her pain.

She threw herself on the bed, face down, upset and unsure how long it would take to find Michelle's killer or if her presence in town would do more harm than good. The only thing she was sure of was that she had to pull herself together and talk to Jordan about how she felt. She couldn't let go of him again. After their encounter, fiancée or not, she knew he wanted her just as much as she wanted him.

Maddie reached into her designer handbag and pulled out her cell phone to call Ally and get advice only a best friend could give. Maddie never came away from a conversation wondering what was really on her mind. Ally's no-filter, straight shooter style was one of the reasons they got along so well.

Maddie was prepared to leave a message after the sixth ring.

"Ally? Hi. I didn't think you'd answer."

"I saw it was you calling so I excused myself from my meeting and left my client with some swatches to contemplate."

"So glad you picked up. You're a lifesaver."

"True, so true," she said in jest. "I've been dying to talk to you. Fill me in. What's going on, girl? Spill."

"Where do I begin?" Maddie took a deep breath. "I'll give you the abridged version for now. First, you know I've kept much of my past here in Timberton from Richard. Particularly Michelle and the whole sordid mess."

"Yes. With good reason," Ally said. "Go on."

"Detective Hanoy called me to tell me Michelle's body has been found."

"Seriously?"

"Yes. So I had to tell Richard about everything...well almost everything because Roger, Detective Hanoy, asked me to come to Timberton.

The department is reopening the investigation as a homicide and he thought I could be of some value."

"Oh, Maddie, I'm so sorry. How are you doing with all of this? Brandon, your dad and, oh crap, your mom?" Ally asked.

"Not good. To all of the above. Richard and I had a big fight about it. He nearly punched me in the face, but stopped short."

"What? You've got to be kidding! You mean literally almost punched you in the face?"

"Yes, literally. He's had his bad days and we've had some arguments, but nothing like this. You should have seen the look in his eyes. He was incensed. A crazy man."

"Did you mention Jordan's name by any chance?"

"Well, yeah."

"There you go. Mystery solved," Ally said. "It wouldn't take Sherlock Holmes to figure that one out."

"I wasn't sure I was going to come, but he made the decision for me."

"Have you seen Jordan?" Ally asked, well aware that she still carried a hot flame for the guy, not that she blamed her.

"Oh yes, and he's hotter than ever. Sexier than I could have imagined. And we nearly fucked in the hay next to a horse named White Shadow," Maddie blurted out with a swift smack to her own forehead.

"What?" Ally laughed at her humorous delivery.

"We were stopped by only one thing. The arrival of his so-called fiancée."

"You're kidding me, right?"

"All of that is a story for another day, although it's killing me to have to put that aside for now."

"You're going to make me wait? C'mon."

"I'll tell you everything, but first I need your right-side brain to weigh in on something. When I was with the detective earlier this evening at a townie hang out called Peg's Diner, in comes this dude, Colin Stone. I may have mentioned him to you. He was the boy who used to be obsessed with Michelle and one of the people the detective questioned when she first disappeared."

"Yes, I do remember. You mentioned you never liked him and he was a super creepy guy."

"Well, as soon as he saw me sitting in the booth, he turned and ran out of the diner like his boxers burst into flames."

"Why would he do that?"

"Exactly. I don't know. He looked crazy, but there was something else. Our eyes locked in on each other. I've only seen that look in the eyes of one type of person, a guilty one. I think I have no choice but to stay and see this through to the end."

"Oh, so you've decided?"

"Yes. And I have a plan."

"Oh boy, okay," Ally braced herself. "Go on. Let's have it."

"Colin lived with his mother and father on the other side of Timberton Lake, not all that far from my parents. I'm going to take a ride to the lake and take a look around."

"Oh for goodness' sake, Maddie. You are a lawyer, not a super sleuth detective."

"Well, lawyers are kind of super sleuth detectives in a way."

"I think you should leave that up to the police. You are gonna get yourself into big trouble. You're too emotional, too close to it. You know what I mean?" Ally insisted she rethink her impulse to take over. "Plus, it could be dangerous. Didn't you say that kid's family was nuts? The father went crazy or something? I'm pretty sure you told me that in the past."

"Yeah, the Stones were as crazy as they come."

"I hate this plan of yours, but at least bring Jordan with you."

"Jordan? Hmm. I don't think he'll like this plan either."

"Jordan will either jump at the chance to have an excuse to spend time with you or he'll tell you you're the crazy one and to leave it to the cops like I just did." Ally's assessment was right on target.

She laughed at her blunt analysis, true to form. "Point taken. I'll ride to over to Jordan's office tomorrow and see what he has to say."

"Okay, girlfriend. You are a pistol, you know that?"

"Stubborn might be more like it."

"True that. I have to get back to my client. If he looks at his watch one more time, his head will explode right off his shoulders. Call me later and be careful, please."

"Will do. Talk to you later."

Maddie shut the lights off, but sleep was not in the cards. She tossed and turned until the pins and needles in the bed forced her to rise.

"I have to do something," she said as she threw on a pair of jeans, a white t-shirt, and a pair of black hiking boots fit to tackle the wooded brush that surrounded Colin's remote shack.

"No time like the present." She walked down the long, dark hallway to the elevator, fearless and convinced that now was the perfect time to pay a visit to the Stones' house.

To appease Ally and include Jordan in her scheme as promised, she called his voicemail and left him a message. Not what Ally had in mind, but it would have to do. For a split second, the idea of driving to the ranch and dragging him out of bed crossed her mind, but with his *so-called fiancée* in the picture, nothing good would come of it.

Jordan's seductive, deep voice requested the caller leave a message. "Jordan, this is Maddie. I know you're probably sound asleep now, next to what's her face. Listen, I just wanted you to know I saw Colin at Peg's Diner. The whole scene was beyond weird. I'll fill you in later, but something is stuck in my gut when it comes to that kid. I don't know what it is, but I'm going to find out. I'm on my way to his house to take a look around. Talk to you later."

As she got closer to her childhood home near the lake, her firm belly turned to jelly and her faded memories grew clearer. The grand, chalet-style home where here parents still lived stood with pride beyond the trees. As a child, she never appreciated her good fortune compared to others who lived on the opposite side of the lake. The days when her dad used to cook on the grill and Mom prepared all the fixings while Brandon, Jordan, Maddie, and Michelle played water games caused her to drift off and lose focus on the task at hand, but the chilly 2:00 a.m. air reminded her of her purpose.

With the shack in view, Maddie shut down the engine and parked in a small space cleared of trees with just enough brush to hide if one of the Stones peered out of the dilapidated window that faced her. The Stones' peculiar and isolated ways proved them unpredictable. Even the townies didn't know much about them. Michelle was one of the few people who got close to the family, not a surprise since she gravitated toward anyone in despair.

Roger had surmised that Colin still lived in the shack, but recent efforts to track him down were unsuccessful. He claimed no one in town had seen the Stone family for some time, until Colin stepped into the diner and ran back out like a chicken who stumbled into a slaughterhouse.

As Maddie crept her way down the rocky, dirt path, her cell phone vibrated.

"Jordan?" She ducked behind a massive oak with a trunk wide enough to hide her entire body three times over. "What are you doing?"

"What do you mean, what am *I* doing? I should ask you that question, don't you think?"

"I'm at Colin's house. You know…the shack on the lake."

"Yes, I know it," he said. "You should get the hell out of there right now. I mean it."

"Why? Do you know something?"

"I just wish you'd told me what you were doing before you went ahead and did it."

"Why, Jordan? If you know something, now would be a good time to share it."

"Ely, Colin's father, is a son of a bitch. He's dangerous."

"What do you mean? Dangerous how?"

"About five or six years ago, he was hired at the shipyard to haul boxes and he nearly took the eyes out of one of his co-workers' head when he went crazy with a nail gun. Almost damn near killed him."

"What?"

"And that's just the tip of the iceberg. Ely went into town almost every night. Bub's Tavern was his drinking hole of choice. He got shitfaced daily, and assaulted and threatened people left and right. He's a violent and dangerous person. And, I hear his wife Zoe went nuts. Legitimately nuts."

"I know this is risky, but I have to do it. I'll be careful. Besides, Detective Hanoy said he hasn't seen any of them in a while. Maybe no one's even here." She peeked around the oak tree to see if she could catch a glimpse of something or someone, but the clouds dimmed the moonlight and the shack looked as dark as the night itself.

"I wish you wouldn't do this alone, but I know I won't be able to stop you."

"No, you won't be able to stop me, but I like that you care so much." She planted one boot into the ground and crunched the dry leaves under her foot.

"You mean a lot to me. You always have. I think you know that," he answered, sincere and to the point.

"Well, your fiancée wouldn't be so happy to hear you say that."

"Maddie, you—"

"I have to go." The conversation veered down a path better suited for another time. She slid her phone into her back pocket and made her way down the dirt path, careful not to announce her arrival. The closer she got, the more she could see how the already dilapidated shack had deteriorated beyond repair.

Maddie ran up to the window on the rickety front porch and crouched under the rotted sill to stay out of the line of sight. Jordan's comments about Ely put her on notice, a message she'd be foolish to ignore. She grabbed an old, rusty metal shovel that lay nearby for protection just in case she ran into one of them. Maddie raised her head high enough to see over the dirt that was cemented to the cracked window on the right side of the house.

Piles of men's clothes and bags of garbage filled the room.

Damn. Looks like the Stones are hoarders on top of everything else, she thought as she crawled past the front door to the window on the other side. *What Colin must have gone through?* She felt bad for him, much as her sister had.

The next room was dark, but light enough to see that it must have belonged to Ely and Zoe. It was neat and tidy compared to the others. The lip of the beige top sheet folded over a floral comforter just so. A blanket at the foot of the bed laid taught and smooth, each thread undisturbed. The bed hadn't been slept in, at least not on this night.

Still not sure if anyone was home, she crawled to the other side of the house and came up for air only when the opportunity to see inside presented itself.

The front porch wrapped around the edge of the house. Maddie crawled over the large, rotted holes to reach the rear entrance that faced the water. The vantage point gave her access to a mediocre view into a back room. Void of people, the cluttered and dirty space had two torn, twin mattresses placed side by side on the floor. As Maddie managed to crack open the window, paint chips flew into the air like a sharp tool sanded them. With no screen to stop her, she stuck her head in to get an unobstructed view.

"Breaking and entering. Great," she said as chunks of rotted wood disintegrated in her hand when she pressed on the sill to give herself a boost forward.

As she scanned the room, she caught a glimpse of a picture of a girl. The photo was propped up on the floor next to the torn twin mattress. The need to enter this house and take whatever she could find that would help uncover the truth motivated her to proceed. Without any thought to the consequences, she pushed herself all the way inside.

Dust and grime an inch thick covered the floor, but she had no choice but to stay low crawl through it as if it wasn't there. She slithered her way around each obstacle. Cockroaches ran from underneath the piles of junk at the slightest disturbance of the filth. Her white t-shirt soiled and a strange, cold liquid penetrated her boots. A whiff of spoiled dairy, rotten meat, and sweaty gym socks passed under her nostrils. Breathing through her mouth was the only way to survive the stench.

As she got closer, a photo of Michelle emerged from the dark. Even though she was unsettled by the find, she didn't think it all that strange that he'd have a picture of her given their close friendship and fact that the majority of the junk that crowded his room included decades-old video games, high school textbooks, and a pile of tattered Timberton High School sweatshirts.

What struck Maddie as odd was the one and only neat area in the room. The 3x3 space seemed cleared of clutter on purpose. She crawled closer to find three knapsacks lined up in a row. She unzipped the first sack in short strokes. Inside, she found some trinkets, old watches, and a pair of men's size eleven shoes. She unzipped the second one a little faster. Her anxiety built and curiosity peaked. The second sack contained green gym shorts, a hockey puck, and collection of tattered comic books. She opened the third bag with haste. One drag of the zipper exposed the contents. Out popped a pair of girl's shoes, hair ties, and a small, red velvet bag with a drawstring. Maddie grabbed the small bag to look inside, but before she was able to loosen the string, she heard a single creak in the floor.

"Shit." Her heart pounded on the walls of her chest loud enough to give her away.

She grabbed the small bag and stuck it in her front pocket with one hand while she reached into her back pocket with the other to get her phone and queue up 911 in case she was in real danger.

Damn it. My phone must have fallen out of my pocket.

She crawled to a dark corner of the room to shelter. The creaky floorboards throughout the condemn-worthy shack made it easy for her to track the eerie, slow steps. The hinges on the doors of each room squealed as they opened and closed. Each step came closer by the minute. It was only a matter of time before the door to Colin's room would open and reveal her like a mouse caught in a trap.

Maddie knew her only chance to escape was to make it back to the window and climb out the way she came in. She eyed her only exit and judged whether she'd have enough time to make it or whether it was safer to stay crouched down in the dark corner and take her chances.

She stayed still. The steps were too close. No sooner had she finished her thought than the unstable floorboard right outside Colin's room squeaked the loudest. Now only the mold-laden door stood between her and the entity on the other side.

Maddie held her breath. The flimsy barrier opened up just enough for the eerie shadow to look inside. The darkness prohibited any more than a glimpse. The longer the silence lingered, the more still she became.

After what she estimated to be five minutes, the beat of heavy footsteps echoed through the shack once again, each one fainter than the last. When the eerie sound reached the other side of the house, she crawled back out the window with the small bag still in her pocket, her phone left buried somewhere in the filth.

She shimmied against the side of the house and glanced behind her. With no one in sight, she made it out unscathed. Maddie turned to make a run for it and landed in what was the unmistakable vise grip of a strong beast.

"Huh!" She gasped, afraid to look up.

"Maddie. It's me. Calm down," Jordan said.

"You scared me to death!" She shook herself loose, took his hand, and led him away from the front of the house so they would not be seen.

"I had to come. You don't know what you could be up against. You're walking a very dangerous line here." He scolded her like a child.

"I'm not going to disagree with you, Jordan. I don't know about dangerous, but I can tell you that family is messed up. It's filthy in that house and the odor is unbearable." She jumped in the passenger seat of Jordan's truck.

"You went inside? Are you just plain out of your mind?" He slid into the driver's seat and slammed the door.

"Shh." She hit him square in the shoulder. "Don't slam the door. There is definitely someone in that disgusting pit."

Jordan hissed with frustration and headed toward the main road.

"Okay, so you went in," he said. "So what did you see? Did you find anything?"

"Yes. There were three knapsacks lined up neatly in a row. A 3x3 space was cleared out on the far side of the room, squalor everywhere else. There wasn't anything unusual in the first two sacks, but the third had girl's shoes, hair ties, and this small velvet bag," Maddie pulled it out of her pants pocket and held it in front of him.

"What's in it?"

Maddie paused before she loosened the string to revel the contents. "I don't know. I didn't have a chance to open it in there. Let's find out."

Just as Jordan's massive front tires hit the pavement of the main road, Maddie let out a cry that could curdle milk. She grabbed Jordan's wrist with herculean force. The surprise of her adrenaline-filled pull caused the truck veer to the far left, crossing over the yellow line on a road so narrow that one would never think it could sustain two-way traffic.

Without a moment to recoil, Jordan saw a black car with no headlights barrelling around the corner at a high rate of speed. It crashed into Jordan's truck head-on, shattering all the windows. Maddie was thrown out of the passenger side window, cut into shreds from the broken glass. The large, metal beast flipped over three times. Jordan bounced around the tight cab like a bingo ball. The other vehicle disappeared in seconds around the bend.

The truck smoldered and gas poured out of the tank. Maddie, unable to move, lay on the cold pavement motionless and unconscious, but somehow the velvet bag remained clenched in her mangled, bloody hand.

Jordan used his mighty upper body strength to pull himself out of the wreck through the windshield between the crushed metal frame. Blood poured down his face, slivers of glass embedded in his cheeks and neck. He dragged his broken body, one inch at a time, over to where Maddie landed. The rocky pavement scraped his flesh, bits of his own skin left behind with each pull. Soon Jordan succumbed to the acute pain.

"Maddie!" His arm reached for her. Her motionless body was just ten feet away. "Can you hear me? Hang on! Please, God no!"

The seconds seemed like minutes and the minutes seemed like hours. Jordan had no choice but to lay in agony and wait for someone to pass by.

CHAPTER FIVE

Time stood still. The sky gained more light as Jordan faded in and out of consciousness from the blows to the head he sustained while he banged around the rolling cabin like clothes in a washing machine. The pain was fierce, but to his surprise, he no longer felt afraid. A warm mass of air hovered over him that seemed to numb his pain and an inner strength replaced his weakness. He had no control over it.

In the distance, Jordan heard a symphony of sirens. He pried open his eyes despite their unwillingness to comply, pulled his arm out from underneath his twisted torso, and reached out for her. "Maddie! Don't give up! Help is on the way."

"Please help her. She must know." A gentle voice echoed through the air.

Jordan's eyes widened, startled by what he thought he just heard. His head shot to the left, then to the right—still no one. With one last rush of adrenaline, he pulled himself closer. This time he was able to drag himself to her and lay with her until help arrived.

"Maddie, I'm here."

"Jordan, I..." she said, breath faint behind the words.

"I'm here. Don't you leave me! Don't even think about it! You hang on. Do you hear me? "

"Sir, my name is Vic, we are going to help you," Captain Walsh from the Timberton Fire Department said as he knelt next to their bodies to assess their injuries.

"Help her, please." Jordan's head rested next to hers.

In seconds, first responders descended on the scene in droves. Special Agent Zimmer and his team from the Timberton Police Department followed close behind. The area was roped off with precision. The paramedics secured Jordan and Maddie in the ambulance and rushed to the nearest hospital.

The first stretcher barreled through the double doors of the busy emergency room with doctors at the ready. Jordan just watched as a medical team descended upon Maddie like hawks to prey. The team ran beside the stretcher with portable drips on the way to the operating room.

Jordan was placed in a room to wait for a doctor with nothing but time to think. His injuries paled in comparison to hers. His heart filled with love and regret. If she made it through this, he vowed never to let her go again. The only thing that stood between him and their future was the past. He wanted to tell her the secret he'd carried with him all these years, but didn't know how. He could only hope he would have the chance to figure it out. *Am I too late? Will she ever be able to forgive me?*

"Mr. Kingston, my name is Dr. Sampson."

Jordan snapped himself out of a blank stare. "How is Maddie? Madison Pike. Do you know anything yet?"

"No, not yet, Mr. Kingston. It will be a while." The doctor slid the paisley curtain around his hospital bed and the emergency room nurses tended to his wounds.

Some hours went by before the staff moved Jordan to a private room on the seventh floor. Each minute that went by with no word on Maddie's condition felt like punishment for all he had done wrong in his life.

"Jordan," Detective Hanoy said. "Can I come in?" Jordan's fiancée Eliza sat by his side.

"Roger. Come in," Jordan answered as he lifted his hand to greet him, but the sharp pain that traveled to his sternum reminded him of his condition. *Better keep my movements to a minimum.*

"Thank you. If I am interrupting I can come back later." Roger had heard Eliza's sharp tongue as he approached the thin curtain.

"Please sit," Jordan said. "You just missed Larry and Brandon. They stopped in while they wait for an update. Good people, those two. Good people."

Roger removed his signature fedora from his head and placed it on the side of the hospital bed. "Yes, Good people, the Pikes."

"I don't see what's so special about any of them," Eliza said, scowling at the mention of Maddie's name.

"Well, you look a little roughed up." Roger ignored Eliza's vitriol and focused on Jordan, his chest wrapped in bandages and a thick cast on his leg.

"Yeah, to say the least. A broken leg, broken ribs, and who knows what else. I can't list it all. There's a chart right over there." Jordan pointed to a clipboard on the wall. "You can take a look if you'd like."

"I will, son. I'm sorry to see this," he said while he gazed at the floor in disbelief. "Any word on Maddie?"

"No, not yet. But I imagine we'll know something soon," he said. "Eliza, could you give us a moment please?"

"I would rather stay." Her angst festered and grew more resentful. Their contentious argument was temporarily on hold, but the venom that seeped from her clenched jaw sent a message she wasn't ready to give up her fight until Jordan revealed every detail of why he left their bed in the middle of the night to meet Maddie.

"Please. I need a moment with the detective."

"I think I have a right to know everything here, Jordan."

"Please. Just go," he asked. His patience grew tired of her bitchy attitude and lack of compassion.

Eliza picked up her things and left the room without a word. Detective Hanoy gave her a nod as she got up to leave the room, but she did not pay him any mind.

"Hmm. What's going on there, if I might ask?"

"Never mind her. She can be as rude as they come, just like her father. He is a powerful man. If it weren't for my dad in my ear for the past three years hounding me to marry her for the good of Kingston Enterprises, I would never give that girl a second thought. I was foolish to agree in the first place. Now that Maddie has returned, I know what love feels like again for the first time since she left town. Everything has changed. I have changed."

"So, tell me what happened last night."

"Maddie called me little before two a.m. to tell me she was headed down to the Stones' shack to investigate. See what she could find. I woke up shortly after she left the message and I bolted down to the shack right away. I couldn't let her go it alone. Too dangerous. You know how crazy that family is. Colin's father Ely was a violent guy. Rumor has it that his drinking just kept getting worse year after year and he became even more abusive. Maddie doesn't know about any of that. No one really knows what went on in that house."

"Much too dangerous." The detective nodded in full agreement. "What happened when you got there?"

"She'd already gone inside. Someone was home, but she didn't know who it was."

"Did she find anything in the house? Or see anything that looked suspicious?" Roger asked. He pulled a small, white notepad and pen from his shirt pocket.

"Yes, she did. She found a velvet bag in a knapsack in Colin's room. Just as we were driving off the dirt road onto the main street, she opened the bag and freaked out. That's when she grabbed my arm with a vise grip and caught me off guard. She pulled so hard the truck swerved. We veered off into the other lane and before I could get control, a car barreled around the corner and hit us head on, and here we are. I don't know any more than that. I don't know what was in that bag that upset her so much."

Roger jotted down note after note until Jordan recalled everything he could. After a few moments, Roger stopped his feverish scribble and looked up. "We need to find that bag," he said with laser focus. His leaky pen made defined blue inkblots on the page with each tap of the tip.

"She had it in her grip when the first responders arrived on the scene."

"What?" He lifted his eyebrows higher.

"Yes. I remember. It was clenched in her bloody hand. She held onto it for dear life." His sad eyes welled up with tears, a sight not seen very often.

"Remarkable," Roger said, more ink leaking onto the pad.

"Something strange happened out there while I lay still on the road waiting for help to arrive."

"Something strange? Strange how?"

"I know you're going to say it was my imagination, but I'm sure it was something else."

"Go on."

"I heard a voice as plain as day. I swear it was the voice of an angel. It sounded just like Michelle. She begged me to help Maddie."

"I'm listening," Roger answered without judgment.

"I know it seems crazy. It's hard to explain. I feel Michelle's presence every day. And when I heard this plea, I knew I had to do more, something, anything. It's as if this...angel was guiding me to find the truth."

"It could have been your imagination. Or something else," Roger said. He had no real answer for him. He wasn't a spiritual man, but supported Jordan's theories regardless. He saw Jordan had changed somehow, for the better.

"Well, Michelle and I were very close. Closer than anyone realized," he went on to cleanse his conscience. "We had a special connection. Things happened between Michelle and me when we were kids that no one knows about, not even Maddie. In fact if she knew, she'd probably never speak to me again."

"I know you and Maddie were inseparable and the girls spent a lot of time at your ranch. Each had their own horse, if I remember correctly."

"Yes, that's right. Maddie and I were in love for sure. Teenagers in love, hormones on overdrive. You remember how that can scramble your brain. Which makes what I'm about to tell you much worse."

"You don't have to tell me, but I'm happy to lend an ear if it makes you feel better. After all, I've known you since you were a little tyke." Roger gave him a soft punch in his good arm.

"Michelle and I had a special bond." Jordan jumped right in. It was as if the guilt he buried all these years was uncontainable; his words seeped out like air from a balloon and relieved the burden that built up in him. "We had a secret. We agreed Maddie should never know because it would kill her."

"What happened?" he asked with sincere concern.

"It was the beginning of the end for all of us. It all started with one innocent occurrence. Then the second, worse than the first. The third worse than the second. And so on. A slippery slope. It tore us apart. It's the cause of all the womanizing and turmoil in my life that followed Maddie's departure from Timberton. We all paid for it dearly in different ways. All three of us."

"Whatever it is, you're a good man, Jordan. Good man."

"I'm no angel." Jordan paused before he continued. He wasn't entirely sure why he decided to tell Roger his deepest, darkest secrets, but it helped him face the fact that he might never see Maddie again. "Maddie, as you know, was, and is, strong-willed. Stubborn at times. Once she gets something in her head, there is no changing it."

"Yes, that's her for sure."

"I thought I knew what she wanted. I thought she wanted me. She said she wasn't ready, but I thought she was just making excuses. I had every girl in town throwing themselves at me."

"Understandable. You were always irresistible to the ladies. Still are today, if I'm not mistaken," Roger said, based on Jordan's history over the years.

"Yes, I guess I haven't had a problem in that area." He could not deny his dating record was one for the books and he did carry a very high opinion of himself, especially as a teenager. "Well, one night after a football game, Maddie and I went to a party down at Timberton Lake. We raised hell in the Old Timber Yard. Everyone got crazy, drank too much, and wreaked havoc on the old building. Trashed the place."

"I'm glad I didn't know about that. I would have had to arrest you," the detective said with some much-needed levity.

"Yeah, we were hellions, weren't we?" Jordan appreciated Roger's effort to lighten the mood just a notch.

"No comment," Roger said, the words spoken out of the side of his mouth. "Go on."

"Maddie and I found ourselves in a secluded part of the Old Timber Yard amongst the cords of wood. I was drunk and acting like an idiot. She could smell the booze on me from a mile away and didn't like it. I got aggressive and ripped her shirt off. At first, she seemed to like it, but then stopped me right in the heat of it. I couldn't understand why she didn't want it and we fought for what seemed like hours," Jordan said, ashamed of his behavior to this day. "We parted ways that night. Maddie went home and I went back to the Lake with the others. Michelle was there. She saw that I was upset and wanted calm me down. You remember what a kind soul she had. She never wanted anyone to hurt or be upset. She was a fixer."

"I do remember her well. Beautiful young lady, inside and out."

"Yes. She was, and I took advantage of her goodness. I knew she had a thing for me and I used her that night. There is no other way to say it. I backed her up against a tree by the water and kissed her like she was Maddie. I seduced her and we had sex that night, and almost every night for the next three or four months. I can't remember exactly how long it went on. I fought the desire to be with her, but I couldn't have Maddie, so I took the closest thing to her."

"I see." Roger saw the guilt Jordan carried; it was palpable as he spoke.

"Michelle and I grew very close."

"Were you in love with her?"

"No," he said. "I cared for her. I always will. But it never turned into love. Not for me, anyway. One day, Michelle put a stop to it. She said she couldn't do this anymore. Going behind Maddie's back was killing her."

"Did Maddie ever find out?" Roger asked as he made a quick pivot in his seat in response to the noise he heard. Unbeknownst to either of them, Eliza stood right outside. Ears plastered to the door, she took in every word of Jordan's confession.

"No. I was going to tell her everything the day Michelle disappeared." Jordan paid no mind to Roger's sudden shift toward the curtain.

"How did you plan on telling her?"

"Maddie, Michelle, Brandon and I, along with some other friends, all went to Timberton Park that Saturday to hang out. Maddie wanted all of us to go. It was the last time we'd all be together before everyone went their own way. I asked Michelle to leave us alone for a while so I could tell Maddie the truth. Michelle wanted me to tell her. That's when she separated from the group and we never saw her again."

"I see."

"I *owe* Maddie the truth. I only hope I will get the chance to tell her."

Roger and Jordan talked for another half hour or so before he said his goodbyes and left to grab some lunch in the cafeteria on the first floor. He asked the hospital staff to call him the minute there was any news on Maddie's condition.

Eliza entered Jordan's room as soon the detective put one foot out the door. She was extremely pleased to be in possession of the confidential information he'd just shared with his detective friend. Her shift in attitude should have been enough to tip him off that something was going on. Her nefarious intent was as obvious as the red color of her shirt.

Rather than head home as she told Jordan she would, Eliza waited in the hospital with Maddie's father, Larry Pike, and her brother Brandon until Maddie's fate was determined. Her mother, Gail, still could not bring herself to face Maddie after all these years, even in the most critical of times.

Larry and Brandon sat in the waiting room ever since the paramedics brought Maddie in and refused to leave until they knew she had made it through the operation. Eliza, however, had her own spiteful agenda, but used her connection to Jordan and her keen sense of manipulation to convince them she had nothing but the best of intentions.

Larry and Brandon became one with the clock on the wall, hypnotized by the steady beat of the long hand of Father Time, while Eliza read the latest gossip magazines. No sooner did Brandon begin to rise from his permanent seat to get a cup of coffee than the surgeon entered the waiting room with purpose. Brandon and Larry stood to attention. Eliza did not budge.

"Mr. Pike. I'm Dr. Iverson." His scrubs were soiled from head to toe and a surgical mask dangled from his neck.

"Yes, doctor." Larry held Brandon's arm to brace for the news. "Will I have the chance to hold my precious daughter again? Doctor. Please tell me I haven't lost another daughter."

"I am happy to tell you she made it through the surgery."

"Thank you, God!" He raised his arms to heaven.

"She's not out of the woods, however. She suffered a serious head injury and her internal injuries were extensive. The next twenty-four hours will be critical, but she is a strong one for sure. I am optimistic." Dr. Iverson put his hand on Larry's shoulder to reassure him.

"Thank you, I am so grateful to you." Larry and Brandon thanked him twenty times before he turned and walked down the desolate hallway. The white, shiny tiles reflected the fluorescent light that illuminated a path for the doctor who had just saved their beloved Maddie.

Brandon went straight to Jordan's room to give him the update he hoped for, but he was sound asleep from the pain medication. The good news would have to wait a little longer.

Larry and Brandon went home with peace of mind and planned to return first thing in the morning. Eliza, however, saw her opportunity to ransack Maddie's belongings before anyone else had the chance. She slithered around the abandoned hallways of the hospital like a cobra prepared to strike.

Armed with the location of Maddie's private room paid for by Jordan, she waited. When the nurse's station cleared out, she made her move. Eliza opened the brown wooden door wide enough to slide in. The space was large and luxurious by hospital standards. It only infuriated Eliza further that Jordan was more concerned about Maddie's comfort and wellbeing than he was for hers.

The small lights from multiple monitors hooked up to Maddie's body flashed in perfect rhythm. The breathing tube Dr. Iverson inserted down her throat was her only lifeline.

"You don't look so strong and powerful now," Eliza said as she leaned in close to her ear and poked at her frail body. "If I was a different kind of person, I'd…"

Tempted to act, she pulled herself away and carried out her original plan. The pink, plastic bag with the white drawstring that held Maddie's belongings followed her to her room. It hung in the closet with no special protection.

"Hmm. Well, look what we have here?" Eliza rummaged through it and found the small velvet bag she held in her hand for dear life. "This was almost too easy."

"Excuse me, miss!" A man's voice interrupted her sinister thoughts.

Eliza slid the velvet bag into her pocket, the room too dark for the man to see.

"Yes, hello," she said, her dumb blonde act came in handy.

"Miss, you are not allowed to be in here," the shadowy figure said with no forgiveness. "And who are you?"

"I was so worried about her, sir. I just wanted to see if she was okay and there was no one at the nurse's station so I just came in to see her for a minute." Eliza avoided the question. As she stepped out of the darkness, she recognized the man to be Dr. Iverson.

"You'll have to leave immediately," he said, angered by her presence. He flipped through the pages of the chart as if she was not there.

"Yes, of course. I'm truly sorry."

She exited the room without another word and headed straight for the parking garage. Anxious to look in the bag before she got into her car, she fought the urge and thought it best to leave the area in case the good doctor decided to report what happened. She jumped in her sports car and sped off with a head full of satisfaction and a heart full of revenge.

CHAPTER SIX

The moment Jordan's eyes opened, he called for his nurse.

"Helen, please tell me she's okay," he asked as he failed in an attempt to prop himself up.

"Yes, my dear." She cupped his hands between hers just like his mother used to do. After more than forty years in this profession, she'd never been so happy to give good news. "She made it through surgery and is resting in the private room you requested for her."

"Thank God," he sighed. "When can I see her?"

"I don't think she can have visitors yet, but I will see what I can do."

"Please, Helen. I have to see her."

With a pat on his shoulder, she left the room to request clearance to bring a special visitor. While Helen went to find Dr. Iverson, Jordan called Detective Hanoy.

"Roger, good morning, it's Jordan."

"How are you my boy? How are you feeling? Any update on Maddie's condition?"

"She made it!"

"Wonderful news. Have you seen her?"

"No visitors yet. My nurse went to get clearance."

"Ah. Well. Congratulations. That is miraculous." Roger let out a sigh of relief. "I'll be there soon. I should take a look though her things and see if we can find that velvet bag you spoke about."

"I swear, Roger, there was something in that bag. We have to find it."

"I'll do what I can."

"Okay, see you soon." Jordan hung up and shimmied to the edge of the bed. His broken leg, broken ribs, and stiff muscles did not allow him to move any farther without assistance.

Helen came back with news that was worth the wait. Dr. Iverson cleared Jordan to see Maddie, but warned him that she is still weak and not out of the woods.

"You can visit with her, but I need you to be prepared for what you are about to see," Helen said with great concern. "Her external injuries are severe. It might be very traumatic for you."

"I was with her out there, waiting for help to arrive. I think I saw the worst of it." His sharp-edged response took his friend Helen by surprise. "I'm sorry. I didn't mean to be curt. I just need to see her."

"Yes, my dear, I understand and I'm sure you can handle it. I just want you to be prepared. She is hooked up to various machines and she's not yet breathing on her own."

Jordan gave his word to Helen that he could handle it and would not cause Maddie any distress.

"Very well then. Let's get you up."

Jordan used whatever strength he had in his upper body to help Helen get him out of bed and into a wheelchair. His massive chest remained covered by bandages, but the disguise did nothing to discourage the line of young nurses that offered to help Helen get him ready. He tended to gather a harem wherever he went and under any circumstance.

Jordan sat propped up in the uncomfortable vinyl chair with extra-large wheels when a soft, female voice called out from behind the curtain.

"Jordan?"

"Yes, come on in," he said. The voice sounded unfamiliar at first.

The manicured hand of a young woman slid the curtain to the left one ring at a time afraid to intrude. An art deco, blue speckled ring entered first, followed by long, silky, blonde strands of hair.

"Hey, it's Alicia." She peeked in. "Are you decent?"

"Yes! Of course come in." His crushed ribs made his attempt to hug her a complete failure, his muscle-packed arm was no help.

Alicia stepped all the way in. Her striking appearance made him uncomfortable.

Wavy, tousled hair cascaded over her bare, tan shoulders and down to the elastic that held up her tank top just above her small but pronounced breasts. As she stepped closer, their eyes locked onto each other and neither of them could look away.

Her green eyes glistened and widened. She scanned Jordan's chiseled face and grand physique. Even as banged up as he was, he oozed sex appeal. His outward appearance was a perfect match for his deep, confident voice. She now had firsthand, visual confirmation of this unique specimen; she needed no further explanation of why Maddie could never let him go.

Alicia hoped her thoughts were not on full display. She forced herself to break eye contact with him and focus on Helen, who stood to his right.

"Hello, my name is Alicia Carter. I'm a good friend of Madison Pike."

"Hi, Alicia dear. My name is Helen, Jordan's day-time nurse for the duration of his stay here."

"It's a pleasure to meet you, Helen."

An awkward moment of silence followed as Helen shot Jordan a quick look as a mother would. Her expression scolded him for his obvious carnal desires. "Would you like a moment before we head over to see Madison?"

"Yes, please," Jordan said.

"Oh, is it possible for me to see her too?" Alicia asked.

"I think so, dear. I will clear it with Dr. Iverson while you two chat and I'll be back shortly."

Helen slid the curtain open like an accordion and secured it to the wall by its straps. She left the room with one last look over her shoulder to remind him to behave. He got the message loud and clear. Amused by Helen's over-protective concern, he could not hold back an obvious smirk.

"So, Alicia." Jordan flashed a big smile. "You made great time. How was your flight?"

"The flight was good. Except for some bad turbulence that scared all the passengers to death. I thought we were going down." She met his smile with an even bigger one than his. "The thing is I've been so worried about Maddie that I don't know where I am half the time. She is all I think about. I would have been here a few hours earlier, but my first flight was cancelled. The next one left on time with no problem."

"It is good of you to come. I'll be honest, Maddie told me about you, but she and I haven't had much time to catch up since she arrived in town. I don't know much about you, but I can see you are a great friend. You two must be very close," Jordan said with sincerity.

"Yes, we're the best of friends. I don't know what I'd do without her. Maddie always has my back. She is a firecracker, that one. And please, call me Ally," she said as she made herself at home and sat on the edge of the hospital bed. "The front desk told me she was recovering. I am so relieved that she made it through the surgery okay."

Ally managed to pique Jordan's interest in more ways than one. On one hand, he wanted to know more about Maddie's life in New York City. What was her life like? Was she happy? Did she ever talk about her past? About him? But on the other hand, as off limits as Ally was, his manhood reacted to her attractive, 5'5" tight body and artsy style. She drew him in with no apparent intention. He couldn't tame himself.

"How did you and Madison meet?"

"By chance, really. Madison was the lead attorney handling a big civil law suit brought by one of my interior design clients. That's my business—interior design," she said, proud as a peacock. "I design for very high-end buyers."

Without as much as a pause, she finished her thought in one breath. "One of my clients renovated his penthouse in the city and ordered a catalog full of furniture from a shady vendor along with specialty custom pieces. The catalog pieces arrived, but the custom pieces never did. My client put down a $200,000.00 deposit for the custom pieces alone."

"200K! That's some order." He shook his head.

"Yes, it was to be a very unique, one-of-a-kind bachelor pad."

"So you've been friends ever since that lawsuit?"

"Yes, friends in an instant. We get each other."

"Who won the case?" he asked in jest.

Ally answered in the only way that fit her personality. "Obvi."

Her word choice exemplified her style.

Damn, she's cute.

"How are you holding up," she asked as she scanned the exposed areas of his shoulders and legs.

"I'm doing okay. This is nothing compared to what Maddie went through." He looked down at his injuries. "I thought I'd lost her right there in the road."

It was at that moment Ally could see that he still loved her. It was unmistakable.

"Jordan, can I tell you something?"

"Of course, please." His brown eyes turned a lighter shade.

"Madison still loves you. She has *always* loved you. And I don't think there's anything in this world that could change that. Not one thing."

Jordan put his head in his hand and pressed on his temple. Ally just sat in silence. His response wasn't what she expected.

After a few minutes, he looked up at her with red eyes and said, "I wish that were true."

"What do you mean?"

"There is—"

Caught up in the moment, he was about to bare his soul when in walked Helen ready to move the pair out of the room.

"Just in time," he said to Helen. He was certain Maddie would be none too happy that her best friend knew the whole story before she did. Given the depth of their friendship, Ally would be sure to tell her all about it.

"Okay, kids," Helen said with authority. "Let's head over to Madison's room. Dr. Iverson said you could have fifteen minutes, but no more. Her father and brother are in with her now."

"Is her mother with them?" Jordan asked, anxious to learn if she was here.

"No," Helen said. "It is just the two of them."

Jordan and Ally looked at each other, saddened by the fact her mother hadn't come to see her. Both of them were well informed about Maddie's painful and nonexistent relationship with her mother.

Helen pushed the wheelchair; Ally followed close behind. The trio silently made their way to her room, the door left open just enough to get a glimpse of her. From the hallway, Jordan could see a beam of sunlight that peeked in through a small space in one of the two window panels. The warm hue cascaded over her face like a bright ray of hope.

Helen went into the room first to see if Larry and Brandon had completed their visit.

Larry sat at Maddie's bedside, his head down, face buried into the firm mattress. He rubbed her arm for comfort, but was careful not to disrupt the IV and other tubes and wires placed all over her body.

"Mr. Pike?'" Helen said with a soft touch to his shoulder.

Larry looked up at her with despair, choked back the tears, and swallowed his pain before he spoke. A scrambled sentence spilled out. "Is she going to be okay? She doesn't look like she is going to be okay."

Larry broke down before Helen had a chance to respond. He could not stand to see his baby girl suffer.

"I'd trade places with her and my Michelle if it would bring them both back to me."

With the unparalleled compassion Helen was known for, she leaned down and gave Larry a much needed hug. "Mr. Pike, she will be just fine. She is a young, strong, and healthy girl. She will not leave you today. Michelle has not left you either. You can feel their love all around us."

"You are very kind." Larry stood.

"Jordan, and Alicia, Maddie's good friend from New York, are waiting outside. Would you like more time or shall I send them in?"

"Please send them in. I'm okay." He wiped away the sorrow from his face.

"Very well," Helen answered.

Jordan and Ally waited for their instructions. Helen exited the room and extended her arm towards the door. The permission to enter was clear.

"Are you prepared for this?" Jordan looked at Ally to get confirmation.

"Yes, I think so." Her words did not match the fear on her dainty face.

Ally played nurse and rolled Jordan's wheelchair into the room.

Within seconds, Ally let out a gasp loud enough to hear down the hall. The sight of her beautiful, vibrant friend hooked up to wires and drips with miles of bandages stained with blood was too much to bear.

"Ally, I think you should wait outside for now," Jordan requested just in case Maddie could hear her.

"Yes, I'm so sorry. It is just too unbelievable. I love her so much."

"I know. It's okay." Jordan was touched by her genuine emotion and grateful that Maddie had a true friend in her.

"I'll wait outside."

Ally left the room to pull herself together and call home to let Maddie's boyfriend, Richard, know what happened.

Ally left Richard an urgent message and told him about the accident. If it wasn't too inconvenient for him, he might call back to find out how she was, but Ally was the last person who would hold her breath waiting on him. After all, he was an arrogant, self-absorbed, self-centered ass. At least, that was Ally's take on him.

She poked her head into Maddie's room and told Jordan she'd be at her hotel.

Jordan, Larry, and Brandon sat in silence. Maddie's motionless body overwhelmed her father with grief and hopelessness, convinced he would lose yet another child and her mother would not have the chance to say goodbye. After five minutes passed, Larry couldn't sit any longer. He became unsettled and paced the room.

"Are you okay?" Jordan asked. He knew at least in part his agitation was because Gail was not here with him.

"I need to take a walk," Larry said as he gathered his things. "Watch over her for me, will you?"

"Of course." he answered. "I'll protect her at all cost."

Jordan took a moment to see if he could find the velvet bag in her belongings. He rolled his wheel-chair across the room to the closet and tugged on the pink plastic bag hard enough to break the draw-string from the hook.

Confident he was about to uncover the mystery behind all of this, he tore the plastic apart until all the items fell out. His disappointment took the air out of the room. No velvet bag.

Jordan wheeled himself over to her bedside. "What did you see? What had you so upset?"

Brandon looked at him, puzzled.

"Can you hear me, sweetheart?" He placed his hand over hers. "I promise you we will find the answers you need and I will never let you go again. Never."

There was no indication that she could hear him, but he spoke to her as if she could.

After Larry and Brandon left, Jordan stayed by her side for hours. He marveled at her courage, read from the Bible left in the room by the priest who'd visited earlier that day, and kept his sorrow to himself so Maddie would not hear the extent of his pain. His love for her multiplied with each caress of her hand.

The silence broke when Detective Hanoy knocked on the door and entered the room.

"Hey there, Jordan. How is the patient?" He limped closer.

"She hasn't moved. No movement at all," he said. "I hoped she would feel my presence and respond to me in some way, but she hasn't even flinched. It's been hours."

"I'm sure she knows you're here. It will take some time. She will be back with us. No doubt."

"I just need a sign. If she could move a little bit I'd… The doctor told her father that her head and spinal cord injuries could cause memory loss and paralysis, but he can't know yet to what degree."

"I'm sorry to hear that. I can only pray that doesn't happen," Roger said.

His rickety legs carried him to a chair in the corner to finish their talk.

"Jordan, we are going to solve this."

"I'm never going to let her go again, Roger. Not ever," Jordan said with conviction.

"Are you going to tell her what happened between you and Michelle? Clear the air?"

"Yes, I'm gonna have to. I don't know if she can forgive me. I can't even forgive myself. But I am going to earn her trust and keep her in Timberton where she belongs."

"Where are her personal belongings? Have you gone through them yet?"

"Yes, nothing there."

"What? Nothing?"

"Nothing out of the ordinary. The velvet bag isn't here."

"How is that possible?" Roger grimaced on one side of his mouth. "Okay, I'm heading over to the Stones' shack again and take another look around."

"Be careful, Rog. Do me a favor, don't get yourself killed," Jordan said. The statement carried some truth under the circumstances.

"Yeah, I hear you. I'll do my best."

He exited the room more pensive than when he'd walked in. Jordan figured it would be at least a couple of hours before he heard from him again. In the meantime, Jordan put all of his focus back onto Maddie.

He spoke to her about the things they used to do when they were kids as if she were able to hear him. He recounted the good times they used to have at her parents' lake house and their first kiss behind the stables at the ranch on one hot summer night.

"I am so sorry for what happened to Michelle." He caressed her head, the bandage damp and pasty. "I loved you then and I love you now." His head rested on his massive biceps that bulged upward as he extended his arm to touch her.

It was at that moment Jordan felt Maddie's body shake.

"Maddie, can you hear me?" He begged her to speak. "Can you hear me?"'

Despite the lack of control over her movements, she slid her right arm over to the edge of the bed just enough to put her hand onto his and then stopped. It was as if she heard what he said and wanted to comfort him.

"Nurse! Helen! Somebody, come now!" He pressed the red call button.

No one answered. As his rage escalated from the lack of a response, he propelled himself up out of the wheelchair without a single thought to his pain, and hobbled to the doorway. His broken leg dragged behind him like it was nothing but a mere annoyance.

"I need someone in here now!" He stood at the door with the authority of a five-star general.

All the staff within earshot hopped to it at the sound of his order. Helen saw all the commotion and ran down the hallway to the room as fast as her old legs would carry her. The room filled up with nurses and aides at all skill levels. The young interns ran in only to observe Jordan in action, a noticeable, unwelcomed distraction. With no time to have them removed from the room, he ignored their inappropriate behavior and told Helen what he saw.

"Her body shook like a wild animal that was just captured. She moved her arm far enough to put her hand on mine and then the tremors stopped." He pointed to her arm and imitated the movement.

"Karen, page Dr. Iverson. Stat!" Helen gave the order to the young intern who abused Jordan with her eyes.

The intercom page echoed throughout the hospital halls. "Dr. Iverson to East Wing, Room 751, seventh floor. Stat. Dr. Iverson—stat."

Helen and her team of nurses worked on Maddie with urgency and skill. Jordan did not have a medical background, but he knew this was no small thing. He exited the room to make space for the staff to do their job. Once again, he found himself at the mercy of something bigger than himself.

Larry and Brandon were notified of the incident and hustled down the hospital corridor toward Jordan like a bull was on their heels. Still no sign of Gail, Maddie's mother, despite Larry's effort to convince her to come.

"Jordan, what the hell happened?" Larry said in a panic.

"I was sitting at her bedside just talking to her and her body started shaking uncontrollably. I called for the staff right away. They're in there now."

"Oh God, help us." The fear caused Larry to bend over like a pro boxer who just absorbed a solid jab to the stomach.

"Hey, she's going to be okay. She is in good hands in there and God is watching over her. You know that." Jordan said.

Brandon helped his father walk over to waiting room until the team came out with a report.

"I'll get you some coffee, Dad. Wait here and I'll be right back." Brandon gave Jordan a nod, a signal to watch his father while he goes to the cafeteria.

Meanwhile, Roger arrived at the Stones' shack to look around.

"Here goes nothing." Roger navigated the termite-infested fence. "Up and over."

With one swift swing, he lifted his crippled leg over a low barrier, one that most people tackled with a small bunny hop. It did not look like anyone was home, but he couldn't be sure.

The trees and shrubs near the shack were overgrown, and the branches hung down like a coven of decrepit witches arms. The walk around the shack was like a hike through a tropical jungle with bugs that swarmed around the rancid carcass of a small, dead raccoon.

I'll be damned. "What got at that poor animal?"

With no real choice, Roger stepped over it. Pieces of the dead animal attached to the bottom of his boots. Unaffected by the foul odor, he continued with a slight push of the ripped screen door that came off its top hinge.

He stuck his head in and announced his presence. "Hello there, anybody home? Did I hear someone say come on in?" he said with a belly laugh. One thing Roger always had was a good sense of humor. He laughed at his own quips most of the time.

As he made his way through the house, he noticed one distinct characteristic that was very different from the description Maddie gave to Jordan. She told him the house was filthy and cluttered. The spaces where he walked were eerily clean and tidy, a far cry from the look of the old, rundown and dilapidated exterior. However, a stench comparable to a football team's sweaty socks after a game in July suffocated him.

Roger continued through the shack. He was curious to find Colin's room and the knapsacks Maddie found. Despite the clean appearance, every floorboard creaked and the unexpected cleanliness could not cover up the deplorable condition of the house.

He looked for a room that fit the description Maddie gave, but not one room had any of the items she described. Someone, somehow, had the foresight to tidy up and make some changes.

"I'll be damned," Roger said as he exited the property to head back to the station. "I'll be double damned."

CHAPTER SEVEN

"Welcome back, Mr. Kingston," his young twenty-something receptionist said as she struck a pose from behind her desk to greet him and show off her well planned outfit. Jordan's return to work was a big event for the ladies.

"Good morning." He made her swoon with two words.

Within seconds, the staff swarmed around him with offers to help him get situated. Only two weeks since the accident, a large cast covered his leg and crutches maintained his balance. "Can I get you some coffee?" an attractive female intern asked. Her name escaped him. "I know just the way you like it."

"I'll go grab you something to eat across the street. You must be hungry after all you've been through," another female intern offered. He had no recollection of her.

Before any one of his eager helpers broke a five-inch heel, he felt like he should say a few words to keep some order. "I appreciate all of your help this morning." Jordan was a magnet. The more he spoke, the more hypnotized the girls became. "I'm fine. Please go back to work and give me your all. That's how you can help me."

The girls stood at attention until he disappeared behind his solid cherry-wood office door.

"Hey there, Big K! Welcome back, you handsome bastard," Frank Malone said, a workplace buddy and newly minted Vice President of Commercial Development. He patted him on the back and followed him into his office ready to update him on the time-sensitive projects that needed his immediate attention.

"Hey, Frank. Good to see you. Come in. Have a seat." He shut the door behind him.

Frank sat across from Jordan and filled him in on the good and bad for each project in the works, but Jordan just sat with a blank stare. His only thought circled around 3:00 p.m., the hour Maddie was scheduled to be released from the hospital.

"Buddy, are you okay?" Frank asked. He wondered if Jordan needed a little more time off to recuperate.

"Yeah." He leaned back in his palatial, black leather chair. A pencil twisted in and out of his fingers before it missed a digit and tumbled onto the desk.

"Are you sure? You looked a little pissed, if you don't mind me saying."

"No, I'm good," he answered with a big sigh and decided to share more with his friend. "It's Madison."

"That's the girl who was in the accident with you, right?"

"Yes, that's right."

"The girls in the office made it their business to find out all the fine details about what happened to you and who you were with. You know which ones they are, nosy as hell."

"Hmm. They should spend more time working and less time monitoring my affairs." He was not flattered or amused by his employees' behavior.

There was a moment of silence before Jordan looked up at him and continued. Frank knew him pretty well even though they had not moved their friendship beyond workday lunches and the occasional office party.

"Keep this just between you and me, okay, Frank?"

"Sure, pal. No problem."

"Madison is an old friend of mine. Well, to tell you truth, she was more than just an old friend. There is history between us. Some good, some not so good. Long story short, she means the world to me. She was hurt bad. It kills me to see her suffer."

"How badly was she hurt?" he asked with deep concern. Everyone in town knew Jordan was engaged to Eliza. No one dared to express his or her dislike for her since her father held so much influence in town and abroad.

"Maddie was thrown from my truck's cab when it rolled over several times and she smashed her head on the pavement with brute force. She was banged up pretty bad."

"Oh, man. I'm sorry, dude."

"She suffered a traumatic brain injury that has caused retrograde amnesia."

"That sounds awful, man. A brain injury?"

"Yes, and as bad as that is in and of itself, the amnesia is going to impede the progress of the investigation into her sister Michelle's death. Maddie can't remember what happened right before the accident. She has some vital information we need but may never get. It looks like she lost somewhere between an hour and an hour and a half before the crash. That time period is key."

"Wait, Madison is Michelle Pike's sister? The sister of the young girl our construction crew found buried in the dirt when we excavated the Old Timber Yard to expand the park?"

"Yup, twin sister," he answered. He picked up the yellow pencil from the desk and tapped it on the edge of his solid cherrywood desk three times.

"That's unreal," Frank said as he slapped his forehead in an effort to wrap his head around the latest news.

"Madison is being released from the hospital today," Jordan said.

"Hey, if there is anything I can do to help, just ask and I'm there."

He took a minute to think it through and decided to take Frank up on his offer. "In fact, there is something you can do."

"Yeah, anything. What do you need?"

"Would you mind giving me a lift to pick her up and drive us over to the ranch? I want her family to surprise her with a big welcome home when she walks in the door." Jordan decided she would recover at the ranch. Neither Maddie nor Eliza had any say in the matter. "And you should stick around for a while. We're going to get her settled in and have a nice dinner. I'll introduce you to some great people tonight."

"I'd be happy to, man. Of course. Yeah," Frank said, honored to help out and even more honored to attend a private gathering on the well-known, sprawling Kingston Ranch. "Let me know when you're ready to leave and I'll pack it up for the day."

"Thanks, buddy," Jordan said, then proceeded to dig into the business matters waiting for resolution upon his return.

Frank exited his office with a new sense of rank on the friendship scale. He could not help but feel privileged that the boss felt comfortable enough with him to let him into his personal life. This was the only time he knew of that anyone from the office had been invited to the ranch with the exception of one office Christmas party held there seven years ago. Frank hadn't worked for the company then, but longtime employees talked about the grandeur of it all and would die for a repeat performance.

Jordan and Frank left the office at two o'clock. A late arrival was not an option. Construction under way caused traffic to back up, but the anxious men made it with fifteen minutes to spare.

The East Wing, Seventh Floor of the hospital had all the action. Helen dressed Maddie and helped her into a chair to prepare her for her discharge. She could walk on her own, but hospital rules required her to leave in a wheelchair for safety reasons.

A soft knock on the door of Room 751 brought a big smile to Maddie's bruised face. Despite the jolt of pain her smile sent to her temples, it stretched from ear to ear.

"Hey, there, pretty lady," Jordan said as he peeked in. His delicious musk entered first, and his crisp, well-groomed appearance established that he'd come straight from the office. "Are you ready to go?" He hobbled over and leaned down to kiss her on the forehead.

"Very ready," she said and inhaled his scent.

She mesmerized him. He saw no one else in the room. It took five minutes before he acknowledged Helen, who stood off to the side. "I apologize for my rudeness."

"Please, dear. No need to worry your handsome self about it. At my age, I've seen it all." Helen proceeded to escort Madison out of the hospital room and toward the elevator.

"Maddie." Jordan snapped out of his trance and introduced the man who walked next to him. "This is my friend Frank Malone from the office. He's going to give us a ride back to the ranch. Larry, Brandon, and Ally will meet us there."

"Nice to meet you, Madison. I wish it could have been under better circumstances."

"Nice to meet you too, Frank. It's sweet of you to help us out today. Thank you," she said with a somewhat coherent delivery.

"Anytime." Frank looked at Jordan with a nod of approval and a good old boy punch in the shoulder to let him know he'd hit the jackpot.

Frank drove with care. He avoided every pothole in the road and made sure he did not drive one mile over the speed limit. As soon as the front wheels of the car hit the newly paved entrance to the ranch, his jaw dropped in awe of the tall, wrought iron gate embellished with grand letters KINGSTON HORSE RANCH. The gate opened to welcome them like the arms of a loving mother.

Frank's new, flashy ride was a formidable contender among Jordan's collection of luxury cars that adorned the circular cobblestone driveway. Majestic, evergreen trees lined the path that led to the front door and the manicured landscape took the breath away from every visitor. The sight of Jordan's prize-winning Arabian horses that galloped free in the pastures made his head pivot in every direction.

On most days, Jordan used the side entrance, which was not as grandiose, but he wanted Maddie to know she was his queen, his purpose. The red carpet that cascaded down the front steps gave everyone that clear impression.

Frank's jaw remained open and ready to catch flies. He was in awe of the life his boss led outside of the office and touched by the gentle heart that lived inside the tough, brawny exterior. Jordan was always happy to provide a sanctuary for his friends and a safe haven for kids who came from all over to ride his horses. The gift of a child's smile and joyous laugh meant he'd given them at least one afternoon where they didn't feel sick or have to think about their illness.

Soon the large K on the front door disappeared. Judge and Jury, Maddie's two precious pups Ally brought from her New York condo, ran outside to greet her with much needed affection. Ally followed close behind in a black, skintight minidress, and sky-high heels that most girls couldn't even walk in. Her unique skill allowed her to stop her forward momentum on a dime. She nearly knocked Maddie to the ground with her enthusiasm and could have crushed the pups that clung onto Maddie's leg with no sign of letting go. Ally gave her a squeeze that could pop a stitch or two.

"I am so happy you are home!" She held her head between her hands in disbelief and cried like a hungry baby.

"Hi, Ally. So glad to be home. Thanks for bringing my babies. Love you forever," Maddie winced a bit from the pain inflicted on her ribs by the embrace, but she wouldn't change a thing.

"Love you too!" Ally said as she wiped away the tears mixed with jet-black mascara. Frank watched the exchange with his jaw still fused open. He pinched himself to be sure this was all real.

The girls turned to walk up the wide slate steps covered by the bright red carpet like movie stars at an award show. On the way up the stairs, Maddie looked at Ally and asked, "Mom?"

"No," she said.

Meanwhile, Jordan and Frank stood while everyone else smothered Maddie with a grand welcome home.

"I just want to thank you for the best day of my life," Frank said as he spread his arms as far apart as he could and reached up to the sky.

Jordan laughed and pushed Maddie's small suitcase into his chest. "Here, take this."

Frank let out a huff as the baggage landed on his pecs. "No problem, bro."

The two handsome men made their way inside. Frank's appreciation for his new best friend continued to grow. The ultra-high ceilings and circular staircases were grand and impressive. The living area with two red brick fireplaces gave off the scent of a traditional wood-burning fire that overloaded his senses.

"Miss Camilla, could you please bring out the hors d'oeuvres for our guests when you have a moment?" Jordan asked his longtime housekeeper who has been with the Kingston family for almost twenty years.

"Yes, Mr. Jordan," she said. "I'll get them right away."

"I want to welcome Maddie home and wish her a speedy recovery. Thanks to everyone for being here. It means a lot to me. I don't know what I would do without all of you." Jordan raised his glass filled with plain soda for now while Maddie toasted her friends with a glass of juice.

After a long afternoon, she said her goodbyes and excused herself from the group. Jordan kissed her on her forehead and walked her upstairs to rest in the room Miss Camilla prepared for her. The new oasis was adorned with soft, white linens, pillows of all shapes and sizes and a puffy, pink comforter that would relax any weary body. It was fit for a queen, just as Jordan wanted it.

The lavish sanctuary was located on the opposite side of the ranch from Eliza and Jordan's room. Even Miss Camilla knew this arrangement was going to be trouble, but Jordan wasn't going to have Madison recover anywhere else. He wanted to keep an eye on her at all costs.

While she rested, Jordan took the others for a walk around the grounds. Frank was especially pleased about the tour so he could use the seductive allure of the ranch as an aphrodisiac and entice Ally into a little fun—his plan from the minute he saw her.

Jordan was the perfect host. Once his guests were well into the grand tour, he left Brandon to finish the rounds. He returned to the main house to check on Maddie and found her face up, immersed in the fluff of the covers with little on but a white tank top and tiny, pink panties. An imprint on the crotch read *Kiss me here.* An order he wanted to follow.

He stood in the doorway, his broad shoulder against the doorjamb. The sight of her long, lean legs and perfect figure weakened him. Her tiny t-shirt shimmied up over her breasts and challenged his self-imposed commitment to respect her space and behave. Despite his best effort to stay the course, his manhood stiffened in an instant and drew him in like a missile to a target.

He entered her bedroom and sat on the side of the bed. His well-muscled frame made a prominent dent in the mattress and moved the bed no matter how careful he was not to disturb her.

Her seductive scent surrounded him. His desire grew more obvious by the second. He wanted to feel her, taste her, and show her how much he cared for her, but he knew it was not the right time.

Unable to tame the lion, he stroked himself while he watched her sleep. She rolled from left to right, her movements exposing herself to him. He wanted to be inside her more than anything he'd ever wanted.

"Maddie?" He said her name a few times before she woke to the sound of his deep voice.

His inflection sent tingles down her back.

She looked up at him with lust-filled eyes and tugged on his forearm with her right hand, a clear message that she wanted him. He followed the line of her body with one finger and cradled her head with the other hand. A simple, gentle kiss on her forehead told her he was there to comfort her and protect her. She knew from that moment on everything would be okay. Jordan stayed by her side and nestled his head next to hers until she fell asleep again.

With one more kiss, he pulled the comforter up to her chin so she could smell the sweet aroma of the special softener Miss Camilla used when she washed the linens. He knew Madison loved the smell of all kinds of flowers when they were kids. The scent calmed her and brought her peace. He only hoped that remained unchanged.

Jordan went downstairs and hobbled his way into the grandiose living room. He sat alone until the others returned from their guided tour with only a scotch and soda to keep him company. He enjoyed the down time and took a deep breath every few minutes to inhale the aroma of pumpkin spice that emanated from the kitchen. Miss Camilla's Timberton Festival award-winning muffins never disappointed. With her secret family recipe handed down by her grandmother and her extraordinary culinary skill, her creations won the Festival Baking Contest every year.

"When are you going to go into business and sell those muffins, Miss Camilla?" Jordan flashed a coy smile. He toasted her with his scotch and soda as she came out of the kitchen to see if the others had returned.

"Oh, I don't know about that, Mr. Jordan," she said, more than a little embarrassed. "That's a big step."

"I will invest in you, you know that." He reminded her of his willingness to back her and help her in any way he could in appreciation for her loyalty and years of service to him and his family.

"You are a very kind man, but I'm happy making them for just you."

"Miss Camilla, you are one of a kind, I'll tell you. Darn happy to have you with me all these years." He raised his glass to her.

"Thank you, Mr. Jordan. You are a good boss... and a charmer," she said on her way back to the kitchen to make sure her muffins were not on fire.

Jordan poured himself another drink and spread his arms out on the lavish sofa with his head laid back and his feet up on the coffee table. His thoughts were lustful, but his love grew stronger by the minute. Maddie filled him up. *How I missed you, my dear Madison. How I missed you.*

The night fell and a strong, cool breeze tugged at the stem of the leaves on every tree that lined the property. The tour group returned when the chill penetrated their bones, but no one wanted to leave the ranch or go inside.

"Come on in and relax. Can I get you all a drink?" Jordan offered as he pushed himself up off the couch and skipped on one leg to get behind the bar to play bartender. "I can mix some pretty mean drinks. Any takers? Larry, Brandon, anything?"

The room filled with a resounding "Yes!" followed by chuckles at the synchronized response. Larry and Brandon followed with a request for some sweet iced tea sans alcohol while Frank and Ally asked for a mixed drink with every brand of liquor in the well-stocked cabinet.

Ally walked up to the tavern-like bar top with the million-dollar view. "This is an amazing place, Jordan." She leaned against the leather edge and stared off into space. The whiff of whiskey that tickled her cute nose snapped her out of her daydream. She grabbed the drink orders, one in each fist, and helped him distribute them to his guests. With his awkward cast and pronounced hobble, the drinks would end up on his shirt for sure.

I could lick it off him. A fantasy she kept to herself.

"Thanks, Ally. This is home. No place like it." He shook the final drink in the tumbler.

She could not pry her eyes away from his biceps until he poured the liquid into the crystal glass. Only then could she break her stare.

"Yeah, this is an incredible place. I would have never moved away," Ally said. "I can't understand how Maddie left this place, or you, no matter what the circumstances. And it smells so good in here. Is that pumpkin spice I smell? Mmm." She walked to the center of the room and handed Frank the stiff drink with a blend of alcohol that packed a fierce punch known to rock the most experienced connoisseur in their town.

Miss Camilla brought out her treats from the kitchen for everyone to pick on while the drinks flowed at a quick pace. The louder the celebration got, the more food she brought out. "Happy stomach makes happy people." She encouraged his guests to eat and soak up the large amounts of alcohol about to hit their liver. Miss Camilla had witnessed many of Jordan's parties over the years: bodies passed out around the pool and bedrooms filled to capacity. He worked hard, played hard, and wanted to love hard. He settled for two out of three, until now.

"Frank and Ally, why don't you crash here tonight? You guys probably shouldn't be driving. There's plenty of room here," Jordan said.

Miss Camilla prepared herself to make up the other guest bedrooms.

"I have to sober up and get going. The missus is probably wondering where I am." Frank's voice emitted a dose of regret.

"You're married? Could have fooled me," Ally said.

"Yup." He understood her surprise since it was obvious he wanted to take her behind the horse stalls and ride her. "My wife is very artistic just like you and I know she would love to meet you. Why don't we exchange numbers and we can all get together, if you know what I mean?"

Ally stared at him for a moment with a curious expression and then agreed.

"Sure, yeah. I would like that," she said, not sure why she agreed to an implied threesome. Despite the fact he was unavailable, she liked him. He was funny and a little awkward. She found herself attracted to his wide-eyed love for life.

"Great, you'll see. You won't be sorry," he said as he pulled out his cell phone like a kid who had just received the promise of a new toy. Seconds after he typed in the last number, he called Ally's cell to make sure she had it right.

"How about you, Ally?" Jordan pressed her to stay. "I'm sure Maddie would love you to be here when she wakes up."

"Really? Yes, I would love to stay," she answered with a slight bounce on the sofa that showed her excitement.

"I'll send someone to get your things from the hotel," he said as he picked up the phone ready to make arrangements at the press of a button. "Oh, and Miss Camilla, could you please fix a room for Miss Ally for the remainder of her time here in Timberton?"

"Yes, of course, Mr. Jordan. Right away."

Miss Camilla made a mad dash to the laundry room to retrieve the sheets she washed that day and ran upstairs to make up the room next to Maddie. She wanted to make their, good friend feel at home and as comfortable as possible.

Almost on cue, Larry, Brandon, and Frank said their goodbyes for the night.

"Thanks for watching over my little girl." Larry shook Jordan's hand with a firm grip to let him know how much he appreciated all he was doing for her.

"Of course, Larry. You know I'd do anything for that girl."

"I know, son. You're a good man. A real good man," he said with a few pats on the back. "I reckon I'll stop by tomorrow, if that's okay? See how she's doing?"

"Yes, please. Anytime at all."

"I want to see if I can persuade Gail to come by with me. I don't know if I can, but she's her daughter too, after all. It's been way too long, time to bury the hatchet, I'd say. You never know when the good Lord is going to call you," Larry said as he looked down at the marble letter K inlay in the floor and squeezed the Scaly Cap that he carried in his hands.

"Of course. Please bring her by."

"'Night, Mr. Jordan." Brandon turned and tipped his wide-brimmed cowboy hat.

"'Night, buddy. See you tomorrow. It'll be all right."

Frank followed Brandon out the door happy as a pig on a vegan farm. "Thanks for an awesome night," Frank said with a grin that spanned the width of his face. "See you at the office tomorrow?"

"Thanks to you for all your help." Jordan watched him to make sure he was sober enough to drive. "I won't be in tomorrow, but call me if anything comes up. You can reach me here."

"Okay, will do, pal." He walked to his sleek ride with a steady step.

Jordan closed the majestic door behind him and turned to Ally. "I hope you will be comfortable upstairs. You're in the room next to Maddie. I think you'll like it. The view is fantastic." He pointed her in the direction of the stairs. She needed a little help to find her way.

"I'm sure I will. Thank you."

"All right. If you need anything, Miss Camilla will be happy to get it for you," Jordan said as he cleaned up the empty bottles of booze and crystal glasses that took over the living room.

"What are you doing?"

"What do you mean?" He looked up at her and laughed. "It's almost two a.m."

"C'mon. Let's just have one more drink." She lifted her skirt up over her red thong and spun around to taunt him with her impeccable ass.

"Ally, what are you doing? Put your skirt down. You're drunk."

Even Judge and Jury, who lied quietly at the foot of the coffee table, popped their heads up and growled in disapproval.

"What? I don't know what you're talking about," Ally said as she plopped down on the plush sofa. "C'mon. Have one more drink with me."

"You know Eliza will be home soon from a bachelorette party, probably shitfaced. And she will be none too happy to walk in on this, which is all wrong on so many levels. You know that, right?"

"Walk in on what? We are just talking."

"Okay, just talking. Let's make sure that's all it is."

"I'll behave. I promise." She dragged her pointer finger from her ankle all the way up to her inner thigh.

"Ally. Stop. Don't do this."

"Okay, okay. I know. You're right, I'm sorry. You are just so hot," she slurred and shook her head in frustration. "I don't know what I'm thinking. I've had way too much to drink. I love Maddie. She is my BFF forever and you're *hers*. That means totally off limits forever in BFF terms."

"I'm *hers*?"

"Oh yeah. You are. You are always on her mind even though she won't admit it. You've been on her mind constantly; all these years...you don't even understand." She caught herself before she babbled her way into more trouble. Impressed with her own ability to snap out of her haze, she closed the subject. "Yup. Yup. That's how it is. So where did you say Eliza was?"

"Eliza went to a bachelorette party for one of her friends," he said as he mixed her another drink, but this time fruit juice was the main ingredient.

"Will I have the privilege of meeting her?" Ally gave him a sarcastic smirk.

"I'm sure you will."

"Fine," she acquiesced. She wanted to stay up and drink some more. "Do you love her?"

"Love who?" he asked, not sure if she meant Eliza or Maddie.

"*Eliza*. Duh."

"Let's just say she grew on me."

"*Grew on you?*"

"Yeah."

"Okay, what the hell does that mean? I'm drunk, don't forget. You have to explain things to me right now," Ally said with her legs spread wide open, but this time unaware of her position.

"Okay, Ally. I think it's time for you to get to bed. Let's call it a night."

"Uhh. Fine," she said. "Where did you say my room was again?"

"Here, I'll help you up." Jordan put his arm around her tiny waist and guided her little body up the stairs with one arm. He opened the door to the lavish, well-prepared room that she would call home for the near future. "Are you okay to get undressed and into bed?"

When Ally failed to reply or make any noise at all, he sat her down on the edge of the mattress to make sure her lungs still functioned properly. It would not be the first time one of his friends succumbed to the perils of too much alcohol and needed medical attention.

"Hey, Ally? Are you okay?" He caressed the side of her face and his mouth hovered dangerously close to hers as if he was about to give her a passionate kiss, but he had no other purpose than to make sure she was still breathing.

Almost unconscious, she leaned in and kissed him. He backed away and held her steady. Her head flopped to the side and with one final gulp of air she said, "I'm so tired."

Jordan let out a quiet laugh. He pulled back the covers on the bed and cradled her limp body in his arms to place her in the center of the soft haven to rest, clothes and all. "Sleep well, Ally."

He closed the door behind him with no expectation of a reply.

Jordan's only path to the staircase required him to pass by Maddie's room. Her essence pulled him toward her like the gravity of the sun. He stood in the doorway and stared. She looked like an angel, the covers pulled up to her nose. The last thing he wanted to do was disturb her, but he couldn't resist the temptation to touch her one more time.

Only a minute more went by before the squeak of the front door announced Eliza's arrival. Jordan shut Maddie's door and made his way downstairs like a man immune to temptation.

"Hey, Eliza. How'd it go?"

"It was crazy," she said, buzzed and horny.

"Good," he said, more than a little surprised at her good mood given the fact that she knew Maddie would be here tonight.

"Jordan?" She rubbed herself up against him. His bottom lip landed between hers and she sucked it until their lips fused together.

"Yes, I'm listening," he answered as much as he could with his face suctioned to hers.

"I want you. Now. Make me scream like you do."

"Those strippers got you all riled up, did they?" He joked while he caressed her bare back more out of concern for her well-being than desire to feel her skin.

"Mmm, yeah. I've had them in my face all night. None of them looked as good as you, though." She unzipped his fly.

"Uhh, yeah. You think so," he said with a sigh of pleasure.

"Let's go to bed. Now." Eliza took Jordan's hand and dragged him to the bedroom. She pushed him onto his back and removed his blue jeans in one fell swoop. He let her take full control. Not typical for him, but he couldn't bring himself to stop her. His stiff rod and swollen head hit his belly button and encouraged her without any more help.

She shed her red panties, wet from her wild night. Her lace bra released her large breasts just enough to allow for a healthy bounce.

"Do you like what you see?" she asked. Her bra dangled in his face like a carrot in front of a rabbit.

"Yes, I do," he answered, but not without guilt. An unexpected emotion, since she was the one he was about to marry.

The moonlight glared through the window and her flawless silhouette kept him hard despite his emotional struggle. Her mouth explored him with heated breath and a smooth tongue. Lick after lick, he came closer to the finish line. His moans deepened and leg muscles tightened. Right before he gave her what she was after, she impaled herself on him and moved her hips back and forth with perfect rhythm until his juice filled her warm space. He couldn't resist.

He rose from the bed like a giant. He lifted Eliza clear off the bed and dropped her on her back. Her long legs spread apart and his still rock hard missile penetrated her being. With each thrust, he went deeper. Harder. Faster. She begged him not to stop and he complied. With another flip, she landed on all fours. She took in his long, thick manhood while he pulled on her ponytail just enough to let her know he was in control now.

"Do you want more?' he asked as he flipped her over again.

"Yes, give it to me. Don't you dare stop," she said, unable to catch a breath.

"Tell me you want it. Tell me," he demanded and pinned her arms above her head with one hand.

"I want it. Yes. Please. More. Now," she begged.

He lay on top of her as she invited him inside again. He pushed up against her, but did not enter. Her hips rose to him. The higher she rose, the more he pulled back just enough to remain out of her reach.

"Not yet." She was at his command.

On the verge of entry, he dipped in, one inch at a time. Their rhythm was magical. It was as if their bodies were one. It never felt so right.

"Ah, Maddie!" Jordan exploded inside her in complete ecstasy.

"What?" Eliza froze before she became unhinged. "What did you just say, you bastard?"

Numb from the shock, her eyes were soaked with instant tears. She ran out of the room and locked herself in the hallway bathroom.

"Oh shit," Jordan said to himself as he rose from the bed and wrapped himself in a light pink, floral towel Camilla left on the end table for a morning shower. The bath oils and shower gel bottles that she'd placed next to it flew across the room.

"Eliza?" He knocked on the bathroom door. The towel did nothing to cover his still somewhat erect beast. "I'm so sorry. Come on out."

"You son of a bitch. I can't believe you just did that to me!" Her words disappeared underneath a guttural cry.

"I have no excuse. I'm an asshole. I'm sorry. I never meant to hurt you."

"Just go to her. I don't want anything to do with you, you damn fool."

She opened the door and raced past him without as much as one look. He followed her and tried to calm her down. Eliza opened her dresser drawer and pulled out a small, porcelain box she kept in the back of it.

"Here." She threw a small velvet sack at him. The delicate features on her face hardened and swelled. Her big eyes turned into small, red slits. "Take it. I want nothing to do with you or your fucking lawyer girlfriend."

"What the hell is this?" he said as he caught it against his bare chest.

"You know what it is."

"Where the hell did you get this?" He waved the sack in her face.

"Okay, asshole, I'll tell you where I got it," she said as she calmed down for a moment. "I took it... from her hospital room."

"You did what?" Jordan's mood changed from apologetic to anger.

"I took it from her room. I heard what you said to the detective in the hospital. I know everything. All your dark, little secrets." Her teeth chewed on every word. "Okay, yeah. I was going to keep it so no one would ever find it. Ever since she set foot back in Timberton, you have been different."

"Eliza," he said with his hands up in surrender.

"No. I'm done. Take it. I don't care. I have never been so humiliated in my life."

"Eliz—"

"Just don't say one more word. Not one more word."

Jordan tightened the floral towel around his waist and left the room while Eliza packed her things. He walked down the hallway and into an empty bedroom with the velvet bag in hand. As mad as he was at Eliza for lifting the bag from Maddie's room, he was glad she'd given it back, even under such painful circumstances.

He looked inside right away and couldn't believe what he saw. He called Detective Hanoy to let him know the nature of the contents and get him over to the ranch first thing in the morning. At 3:30 a.m., Jordan expected to leave a voicemail but instead, the detective answered.

"Hanoy here." He struggled to wake up and shake off the cobwebs.

"Hey, Rog, it's Jordan."

"Is everything all right?" He spoke just loud enough for Jordan to hear as he pushed his rickety body up from a flat position.

"Yeah, I'm sorry to wake you. I expected to get your voicemail."

"No worries, son. I answer if I can. You never know. It could be an emergency."

"I have the velvet bag Maddie was talking about."

"What? You have what?"

"The velvet bag."

"Well, here's to warm apple pie with vanilla ice cream. I'll be damned," Roger said with shock and awe. "Where in the world did you find that?"

"It's a long story. Can you head over here tomorrow?"

"Yes, yes of course. What's in it?"

"It's a chain and pendant."

"A chain and pendant? Of what?"

"It's the other half of the unity pendant Maddie wears. Their parents gave it to them when they were kids to remind them they are stronger when they come together as one. They wore it every day. Never took it off."

"Well, I'll be." The detective slapped his left knee a little too hard in response to the news.

"No wonder she blew a gasket. That son of a bitch Colin had it in his house. How did he get his hands on it?" Jordan said.

"I'll be over early tomorrow afternoon and we'll devise a plan. I have one stop I have to make in the morning, but I'll be there as soon as I can."

"Oh man." Jordan rubbed his brow and tightened the towel around his waist again. "Okay, see you then."

Riled up and restless with only hours left before the apocalyptic day arrived, he crawled into bed alone. With arms behind his head and a blank stare at the ceiling, the pain he had caused Eliza saddened him, but he couldn't help relishing in his passion for Maddie. Despite the guilt he harbored for his part in Maddie's departure nine years ago, he vowed not to let it stand in his way anymore. He wouldn't lose Madison Pike again. That was not an option.

CHAPTER EIGHT

The six o'clock hour came and went faster than Jordan was prepared for. At seven o'clock, he woke to the glorious smell of cinnamon pancakes Miss Camilla was cooking in the main kitchen right underneath the upstairs bedrooms.

She prepared a feast fit for an entire kingdom. Everyone in town appreciated her culinary skills, and her magnificent dishes drew crowds around her booth at the Timberland Park Festival every year. With this year's celebration only a week away, Jordan stocked the kitchen with all the fixings she needed to execute her award-winning menu, a small token of his appreciation for her loyalty and all her hard work.

"Good morning, Miss Camilla." Jordan stretched his arms up to the ceiling and inhaled the scent of sweet cinnamon.

"Good morning, Mr. Jordan." She continued to mix the filling for the pies she had on deck, not one stir out of rhythm. "Did I wake you?"

"Yes, and I love it," he answered. She had his permission to wake him with her cooking anytime.

"Will Miss Madison and Miss Alicia be joining you this morning? I made plenty."

"Yes, I think so. I will wake them soon, but I also would like to call Maddie's father and brother to join us, and extend an invitation to her mother too. Do you think there is enough prepared? I don't want you to go to any more trouble."

"Oh, yes, Mr. Jordan. Plenty. And it is never any trouble."

"Excellent. What would I do without you?" He leaned over and gave her a friendly bear hug. Her face took a dive into his rock-hard abdomen whenever he hugged her due to her short frame. He never got any argument from her on the matter.

"Oh, thank you," she said as she put her hand to the side of her face. "You always make me blush."

Jordan flashed her another smile and poured himself a cup of black coffee. He slid open the glass doors that led to the spacious outside deck adorned with high-end patio furniture and a lavish fire pit that had witnessed some of his most intimate moments.

The sun was bright and the air filled with joy, at least for the next hour.

"If only I could stop time." He stared at the majestic horses that grazed across the spacious grounds without a care in the world.

With that final thought, he took his cell phone out of his jeans shorts, selected Larry Pike from his list of hundreds of contacts, and waited patiently ring after ring for him to answer.

After the eighth ring, a woman's voice filled the dead space.

"Hello?" the woman said with a delicate tone and flat inflection.

"Hello, ah, yes, is Larry at home please?" Jordan was, taken a bit off guard.

"One moment please."

"Hello, this is Larry."

"Good morning, Larry. Jordan here."

"Hey there. How's it going this morning?"

"Good so far. Maddie and Ally are still asleep, but I'm going bribe them with some cinnamon pancakes. That will get them up."

"I reckon that will do it."

"Why don't you, Brandon, and Gail come on over and join us? There's plenty to eat and there are some things that transpired last night that you may want to know about. Detective Hanoy will be coming by soon to discuss what we should do."

"Hmm, well, Brandon and I will come, but I'm not sure about Gail. That's a tough order." Larry shook his head.

"Okay, understood. But this would be a good time to get the two of them together, in the same room at least."

"Agreed," Larry said.

"And Miss Camilla makes a breakfast that will knock your socks off."

"Sounds great. We'll head over…and thank you for caring for my little girl."

"You can count on it, sir."

Jordan went inside with optimism. He grabbed another cup of black coffee and made his way up to Maddie's room to wake her. He reached the top of the stairs only to find Ally walking into the bathroom at the end of the hallway. She wore nothing but a ribbon that held her disheveled hair up in a bun. He struggled to look away, but his feeble attempt was less than honorable.

His best guess was she chose to use that bathroom to experience the twelve-person spa with showerhead lights in every color of the rainbow. The colors flashed to the beat of music from any playlist, a fun feature that tended to amuse his intoxicated guests. Jordan couldn't remember anyone who passed up the opportunity to get their groove on.

"Hey, sweet thing. Are you awake?" Jordan lay next to Maddie's warm body.

"Hey." She yawned and stretched her legs; her salacious hips rose from the bed as Jordan brushed her hair off her face.

"How are you feeling this morning?"

"Pretty good actually. A little weak, but I feel more alert than I did yesterday."

"That's good to hear. The doctor said it would be a little while before you feel like yourself again, but he doesn't know what a fighter you are. Nothing can keep you down for long."

"What about you, Mr. Hopalong?" She laughed and threw him a little jab.

"Oh, yeah? Is that how you want to play this?" He tickled her side and caused her belly to ache from laughter; her feet flailed about and pushed the comforter to the floor.

As much as he knew he should hold his hunger for another time, he couldn't resist completely. He let her have one final giggle before he grabbed her and propelled her body flush against him. His hands cradled the soft crease of her ass to pull her closer. He explored her every inch with a sincere desire to know her, all of her. Her wet panties showed him his message was well received. Before he couldn't turn back, he stopped and laid her back down with care.

"What's wrong?" she asked, confused by the sudden end to their encounter.

"Nothing. I want you more than anything I've ever wanted."

"I'm well enough, if that's what you're worried about. You won't break me." She used her soft baby voice to entice him into picking up where he left off.

"We have guests coming for breakfast and Ally is up."

"She is? Did you see her?"

"Oh, yeah. I did see her all right." He avoided the details.

"So we should get downstairs, huh?" The big-city diva in her wanted to make a case to stay in bed, but the small-town girl in her agreed with him.

"Yes. I think we should."

Jordan helped her up out of bed and left her to get ready on her own. Maddie shot him a look of approval as he shut the door behind him.

About a half hour went by before the breakfast guests arrived. The doorbell rang and Jordan signaled Miss Camilla to keep on cooking. He would answer the bell and escort his guests into the dining area. He opened the door to find a welcome surprise.

"Hello, Larry and Brandon. Come on in," he said as he shook Larry's hand and gave Brandon a nod. "And welcome, Gail. Won't you please come in?"

"Thank you." She hesitated for a moment, her face tilted toward the marble floor.

"Please." Jordan encouraged her to come in farther and guided her toward the living room sofa.

Ally chatted up Miss Camilla in the kitchen and listened to her recite the menu she was preparing for the festival next weekend. The two became fast friends with plans to exchange lessons on cooking and interior design.

The rustling in the dining room was a signal to Ally that others arrived, open season for her. Socializing with anyone and everyone was an activity she never passed up. The label *social butterfly* was an understatement.

"Hi, Brandon. Hi there, Mr. Pike." Ally bounced into the room dressed in authentic ranch attire. "Good to see you again."

"I would like to introduce you to Mrs. Gail Pike, Madison's mother," Jordan interjected so Gail would not feel excluded.

"Hello, Mrs. Pike. I am Ally, Maddie's good friend back in New York City. It's very nice to meet you," she said, cool and collected, but shook in her man-made leather boots at the thought of Maddie's reaction to seeing her mom sitting at the table. Now. Today. She expected it would not go well.

There was no response from Gail. Just a blank stare. Everyone looked at each other, not a word spoken. The message was louder than an announcer at a circus who encouraged patrons to step right up and see the freak show. Everyone except Jordan and Larry thought today's meeting was a bad idea, especially because Maddie had no idea this was coming.

Miss Camilla walked in with food galore, a much-needed dose of good cheer.

"Everyone, eat and enjoy," she said as she brought out tray after tray.

Ally jumped to help her so she could remove herself from the awkward climate in which she found herself. Even Miss Camilla could feel the tension in the room, but pretended not to notice. The quick bond Ally formed with Miss Camilla allowed them to communicate with a simple look on the way into the kitchen.

Jordan put on some soothing country music to lighten the mood in the room and fill the air with some noise. Everyone was eating. No one was talking.

"I love this song," Jordan said as he stuffed a whole pancake in his mouth and a sausage to chase it down.

Finally, Jordan could see Maddie coming down the grand staircase. She looked rested and as beautiful as always. Ally and Miss Camilla placed the last tray of food on the table and caught up with Maddie as she made her way to the dining room.

Fearing her reaction to her mother's presence and the uncertainty of Gail's intentions, the room looked as if everyone had turned to stone. Not one muscle in motion.

As Maddie approached the room, her thoughts filled with images of Jordan and his advances earlier that morning. She turned the corner to receive her biggest surprise yet. There sat the last person she expected to see, her mom. Ally was ready to pass out from the tension that sucked the air out of the room. Larry, and Jordan just watched for a sign of what was to come, and Brandon recited a short prayer with the hope that one of them would say something before dinnertime rolled around.

To everyone's delight, Maddie broke the stare first, walked over to her mother, and hugged her like never before. Gail rose to her feet in stoic fashion. Then within seconds, she melted in Maddie's arms and tears flowed throughout the room.

"I have missed you, Mom." She embraced her with an unbreakable hold.

"Oh, my darling Madison. I am sorry. I am..." She gasped for breath, every word drowned out by pain she'd held in for so long.

Their embrace lasted longer than any they'd ever had. Even Brandon, who always claimed no one would ever see him cry, was moved to tears by their undeniable love.

"We will spend time together and figure this all out." Maddie caressed the side of her mother's face, a face she missed, but felt forced to forget.

"Yes, we have much to say. So much time lost." Gail nodded her head and assured Maddie that she wanted the same thing.

"Let's sit down and have a nice day today, okay?" Maddie said.

"Yes." Gail took her seat and softened. The hard and cold exterior she wore for nearly a decade vanished in her daughter's embrace.

Jordan stared at Maddie and watched the burden of guilt lift from her shoulders. He loved her more in that moment that he ever had.

The tension in the room relaxed and the day filled with great promise. After breakfast, everyone took a walk around the grounds to work off the calorie-packed extravaganza and absorb the beauty all around them. Before Brandon's shift started at the firehouse, he showed his mother all the horses that participated in the weekend riding camps for the disabled children and brought her through the stables to see some of the thoroughbreds.

"How you doing, sweet thing?" Jordan pulled Maddie close against his hip, his arm around her shoulder.

"I think I'm exhausted already."

"You were wonderful in there. So strong. So forgiving."

"Well, gee, thanks." She gave him a playful punch in his eight-pack.

"Hey, listen." He turned her to face him.

"What is it?"

"We have some things we have to address today. Detective Hanoy will be by in a little while. Are you up for it?"

"I suppose so." She sighed. "I still don't remember what happened. It's so frustrating. I only remember driving to Colin's house. And then, nothing."

"I know. It will take some time. You had a severe head injury, but the doctors think your memory will come back."

"Why can't you just tell me what happened?"

"Let's wait until Roger gets here."

"Fine, but I don't like it. You know I have no patience."

"You'll know more soon enough. It won't be easy to hear," he said.

"I don't know if I'm ready, but I want to know what happened. By the way, where is the lovely Eliza?"

"She's gone."

"Gone? What do you mean, gone?" A measure of satisfaction combined with curiosity adorned her face.

"I'll tell you about it later." He put his hand on her lower back, guiding her into the house from the patio.

She could sense that now was not the time to press the issue.

Larry and Gail made their way back to the house and sat on the living room sofa in awe of the manicured grounds and the majestic horses that roamed free. Despite the beauty that surrounded them, sadness for time lost and memories that could have been darkened the bright day.

"Time to look to the future." Larry stood to say his goodbyes.

"Would you like to stay and hear what Roger has for us?" Jordan asked.

"I think we should head home now. It has been an emotional day for Gail. I think you can handle things here."

"Sure, of course." Jordan stood to escort them to the door. He knew Larry didn't want Gail to hear what the detective had to say.

"Mom, having you here today meant everything to me," Maddie said. "I wish you could stay."

"Me too, my dear. When you are up to it, come by the house. Soon. We'll talk," Gail whispered into her ear and fought back the urge to grab onto her and not let go.

"I will, Mom. This week. Maybe before the festival this weekend. Will you be going?"

"I hadn't planned on it, but now...I just might."

Brandon ran inside to say a quick goodbye on his way to the firehouse and Ally returned to the main house drenched and perky after riding one of the horses around the corral. Her jeans short shorts wrapped her figure like a perfect package and soaked the seat she called home for the next fifteen minutes before she went upstairs to change and cool off in the rainbow shower. Her new favorite space in the house.

"What a rush," Ally said as she walked up the stairs, half of her clothes already off. "I could really get used to this."

"You can stay as long as you want," Jordan said loud enough so she could hear, but expected no reply. "She's not a shy one, is she?"

"No, a little crazy, but not shy. I love that girl."

The doorbell rang as Ally passed by the stair landing topless on her way to her room.

"The detective just missed the show." Jordan laughed at the near miss as he opened the door. "Hey, come on in, Rog."

"Good afternoon. Sorry I'm late." He removed his hat.

"No worries. C'mon in. Can I get you some ice water, tea, anything?"

"No, thank you. I'm doing just fine," he said and sat near Madison. "Well, how are you doing, young lady?'

"Hi, detective. I'm okay. Today has been a good day so far. I still can't remember much of anything, but other than that, well enough."

"It will take some time. It will come." He reassured her as a father would. "Has Jordan filled you in on the latest events?"

"No, not yet. He wanted to wait for you. And my parents were here for breakfast today."

"Your parents? As in father and…mother?"

"I know. It's nothing short of a miracle."

"How did that go for you?"

"I had no idea what it would feel like, but as soon as I saw her, I wanted my mother back. Nothing else mattered."

"You are an amazing woman, Madison Pike," he said. "Not that I had any doubt of it, mind you."

"Thank you. You are too kind. I don't deserve that much credit."

"Well, I think you do. Do you have it in you to talk about this today? I can understand if you need more time. Jordan and I can get things started."

"No, I'm good. Let's do this."

"Very well then." He unclipped his notepad from his belt and went from friend to detective in an instant. "I will put this in the gentlest way possible. But I will warn you, some of this may be startling to you."

"Okay," she said. "I'm ready. Let's go."

Jordan sat close to Maddie for support and leaned forward with his elbows planted on his knees as the detective scrolled through the questions he prepared to ask her.

"What is the last thing you remember right before the accident?"

"I remember you and I were sitting in Peg's diner and the bastard walked in. And as soon as he saw me, he bolted like he was on fire. That night, around three or four a.m., I drove to Colin's house on the lake to see what I could find. It's a blank from there." Jordan saw signs of the old Maddie come through. Her toughness and determination returned and the fire in her belly ignited.

"You called Jordan that night and told him where you were. He met you there. You exited Colin's house and told Jordan what you saw." He paused for a moment to observe her demeanor and assess whether he should continue or schedule the rest of the meeting for another time. "There was a knapsack. In it you found something."

"I found something?" she said with no memory of it.

"Yes. Do you remember what it was?"

She put her forefingers to her head and proceeded to think. Frustrated by the fact she couldn't recall anything, she threw her head back and pulled her hair into a makeshift ponytail as if somehow that would help her remember.

"Uh, no. Damn it." She tightened her ponytail. "I don't...just don't know."

"It's okay. It was...a small velvet bag with a drawstring."

Maddie listened, but was anxious for him to get to the point.

"You and Jordan got in his truck to drive away. When you opened the bag to look inside, it shocked you and that's when you put a vise grip on Jordan's arm, the truck veered into the northbound lane, and spun out of control to avoid the oncoming vehicle."

"What?" She rested her head in her hands. "Where is the bag? Do you have the bag? What was in it?"

"Well, it has been found."

"Where?"

The detective looked at Jordan and said, "That will be a story for another time, but we have it."

"Okay, tell me what was in it. Just tell me."

A short pause followed. Then Roger slipped back into friend mode and disclosed its contents. "It was the other half of the unity pendant that you wear around your neck."

"What?" Her voice reached its highest pitch.

"Now wait," Roger said. "I know what you're thinking, but let's use out heads here. There may be many good reasons why Colin had this pendant. You know better than anyone it is not conclusive of his guilt."

"Son of a bitch." She paced the floor and thought like a lawyer, not a sister. "We need to talk to him. Find out what he knows."

"I have an idea," Roger said.

"Let's hear it." Maddie's hands clung to her hips.

"Okay, hear me out," He scooted to the edge of the sofa to deliver his plan. "Let's start with what we know about him from his childhood to now."

"Okay, yes. Shoot," she said in full agreement.

"He is elusive. A virtual recluse. We know his father beat him as a child and he developed serious emotional and behavioral issues. He was mercilessly bullied in school, practically tortured by the kids. Arrested five times; twice for assault and three times for breaking and entering."

"Yeah, and Michelle befriended him," Maddie said. "She was a fixer. She always solved everyone else's problems for them. That's who she was."

"Let's find out what he knows." He flipped open his notepad again. "I'll pick him up for questioning, but we will have to find him first. He's been seen around town, but disappears just as fast."

"He can't be that hard to find, Roger." Maddie wondered why he hadn't picked him up already. "I think I should talk to him first."

"It's too dangerous for you to get involved. We don't know what he'll do if he feels threatened," Jordan said.

"Jordan's right. He could be as dangerous as a loose cannon. You saw the way he reacted in the diner when he locked eyes with you."

"That's exactly why I should be the one to talk to him first. I get a rise out of him. I know things about him. Things Michelle shared with me. I know I can get through to him if I can get him to talk to me."

"She may be right, Jordan."

"Rog, it's far too dangerous."

"I have to be the one to do this," she said. "Colin is involved somehow, I know it…and I am gonna get it out of him."

Jordan rubbed his brow in frustration, but knew he wasn't going to change her mind. Her memory of the accident had not returned yet, but the old Maddie was front and center.

"Okay, fine." He threw his hands up. "What's the plan?"

"The festival. Let's find a way to lure him to the festival next weekend. He'll never suspect an ambush by yours truly." She pointed at her face.

"Are you sure you are up for this?" The detective gave her the raised eyebrow.

"Hell, yes. Let's do this."

"Okay, then." Roger closed his notepad and picked up his cell phone to make the first call to put the plan into motion. "I'm going to set you up with a wire and my team is going to stay close by in case anything goes wrong."

"Fine, I'm good with that," she said without hesitation. "Jordan?"

"I don't like it, but I suppose I can't talk you out of it."

"Not a chance." She flashed him a devious smile.

"I'll be in touch once I get my team up to speed. You and Jordan come down to the station this week and we'll run through it." He grabbed his hat off the sofa and placed it on his balding head.

"Thanks for coming by." Jordan closed the door behind him and watched him through the side windowpane as he hobbled to his car.

"Don't you think it's a bit strange that the he hasn't been able to *find* Colin yet?" Maddie offered once the detective was out of earshot.

"Yeah, I found that to be a very strange comment and it's not the first time he has alluded to that.

Colin has been seen around town here and there. I've even laid eyes on him a couple of times myself."

Maddie gave the detective the benefit of the doubt, given the friendship and kindness he extended to her parents over the years. She chose to dismiss any suspicion that came to mind, but the knot that lingered in her belly was like a sucker punch to the gut.

"C'mon." Jordan put his arm around her and led her outside to calm her down even though he knew no amount of sunshine or green pastures would do it.

Jordan noticed her compressed brow. The thought of her next move consumed her. Despite his need to tell her Eliza was gone, permanently, he knew her well enough to know he had better wait.

CHAPTER NINE

The Timberton Park Festival was now only two days away. The sunshine beamed through the floor to ceiling windows that circled the dining room. Time moved like a snail in anticipation of the first meeting with Roger's team, despite her persistent request to meet earlier in the week.

Maddie was anxious for the big day to arrive. Between bites of exotic fruit and French toast, she finalized the details of their plan so it would go off without a hitch.

"I wonder what Rog has in store for us this afternoon," Jordan said as he paged through the newspaper dressed only in his shorts and flip-flops.

"Roger better pull this together, that's all I can say." Maddie implied she would wring his neck, friend or no friend, if he let her down. "I already have a plan and I intend to execute it no matter what he comes up with."

"I figured as much." He laughed in response to the defiant diva he loved.

"I'm going upstairs to change. I think we should leave soon," she said.

"We're going to be very early, you little spitfire."

His calm demeanor had a soothing effect on her. She shot him a sexy look to entice him to follow her and help her get dressed, but he resisted the temptation until the time was right.

At 1:00 p.m. sharp, Jordan and Maddie jumped in his convertible and headed to the station just a few miles away. It was hard to believe the bright, hot sun that greeted them this morning would disappear tomorrow behind torrential rain and high winds.

As soon as the car pulled into the parking lot a full two hours early, Maddie jumped out of the passenger door and entered the police station as if she owned the place. She captured the attention of everyone in sight with her confidence and stunning appearance. Jordan followed close behind, having the same effect. Their presence demanded attention, and their swagger captivated those in their wake.

"Good afternoon, Ms. Pike," Special Agent Zimmer said as soon as he saw Madison walk around the corner. "How are you? Good to see you up and about."

"I'm doing well, thank you. Still having a little trouble remembering some things, but overall, very well."

"Good to hear."

"Is Detective Hanoy in yet?"

"Yeah, he is. Right over there." Agent Zimmer pointed to Roger's office. "You can go ahead in."

"Thank you." She turned to Jordan and signaled him to follow her.

Roger was on his cell phone. He stood with his back to the doorway, leaning against his desk for balance. Maddie and Jordan stood just outside until he was finished with his call. Not intending to intrude on his privacy, they couldn't help but hear his words that echoed farther than the detective intended.

"You'd better listen to me, Col—" He pivoted on his bad leg and faced the doorway when he saw Jordan and Madison within earshot. It was inevitable that anyone who stood within five feet of him would hear his side of the conversation. "Colleen, I'll have to call you back."

"You're early." He cleared his throat and fumbled his phone.

With one glance at each other, Jordan and Maddie knew they were thinking the same thing.

"We are anxious to meet the team and go over the details." Maddie feigned ignorance.

"Oh, okay. Yeah, that's fine," he said, taken off guard. "Have a seat. I'll see if the rest of the team has arrived and we can get started."

The detective left the duo sitting in his office while he went out to rally his men. His exit was swift and his hobble did not seem to impede him under the circumstances. It was obvious he was unsure of what his guests overheard.

"What the hell was that?" Maddie blurted out in an aggressive whisper.

"Sounded like Colin was on the line." Jordan stood to peer over his desk.

"Exactly." Her tone was as sharp as a razor.

"Let's just see who he really was talking too." He picked up the cell phone he left on his desk in haste.

Maddie guarded the doorway while Jordan scrolled through his recent calls. Lucky for them, almost no time passed between the time he'd hung up and when he'd sped out of the room, so the phone remained unlocked.

"Jordan, hurry. There are people walking this way."

He found what he was looking for, but only had enough time to put the phone back the way he found it and take quick seat.

With no time to put her curiosity at ease, Jordan stood to greet the detective and three well-built officers.

"These are Officers Peterson, Smith, and Ellis." Roger introduced the team with no pause. "These officers will be present on Sunday, ready to jump in if needed, and Officer Troy, who is not here yet, will wire you up, Madison."

"Pleasure, ma'am, sir." A respectful nod thrown Jordan's way.

"I have it on good authority Colin Stone will attend the festival as he has the past few years," Roger said.

"How do you know that, may I ask?" Maddie's suspicion was unleashed, but subtle enough not to put anyone on notice.

"I've talked to a lot of people around town this week and they have reported seeing him at the festival for the past five years or so." Roger addressed the officers to avoid eye contact with Maddie, a fact that did not escape her keen sense.

"I see." Her inflection revealed more doubt. "I think you should leave it up to me to pin him down. I'll pick the right moment to approach him. One where he can't escape me."

Jordan watched Maddie take over the meeting and command the room. The exchange and banter heated up the cold, brick precinct walls. She got her way on every point.

"I think we are done here." She concluded the meeting as if she were their boss. "Thank you, officers...and detective."

"Thank you, ma'am." The men answered in unison a second time, affected by her in every way. Her beauty left an imprint in their minds, but her intellect took them by surprise.

Jordan and Maddie made their way to the parking lot in silence. They knew the conversation they were about to have had to take place away from the station without any possibility of being overheard. He drove them to a secluded area near the lake and parked far from any houses to ensure their privacy with no interruptions.

"We can't trust him." Jordan started right in on the attack. "I can't believe it."

"Who was it? Who was Roger talking to?"

"The most recent call on his phone came up as C. Stone."

"Son of a bitch!" She slammed her fist on the dashboard. "Colleen, my ass!"

"If he was talking to Colin, why lie about it?" he said.

"I don't know, Jordan. It makes no sense. Maybe he wanted to get information from Colin and thought I'd go bat shit crazy on him since I insisted on questioning him first."

"I suppose that's possible, but pretty unlikely."

"Damn it. I can't believe we are having this conversation about Roger. Roger, of all people. I wanted to believe he was a friend. We can't let him know we are on to him."

"I agree," he said. "I can't wrap my head around it. I opened up to him about many personal things when he came to visit me in the hospital because I trusted him. Completely. Now...I'm not so sure that was a good idea."

"What personal things?"

"Never mind that now."

"No, really. What personal things?" Once she got something in her craw, she didn't let it go.

"About us," he said.

"About us?"

"Yes. When this is over, we have a lot to talk about. I will tell you one thing right now. I am never letting you go again." He leaned over and pulled her into his space in one fell swoop.

Jordan pushed the front seat back far enough to swing her right leg over his firm lap and boosted her on top of him. Her face came within inches of his mouth. His tongue examined her full red, lips as he took command and held her hands behind her back. His teeth tugged at each dime-sized rhinestone button on her white cotton shirt.

"Jordan," she groaned.

"Tell me what you want," he asked as his voice deepened. "Tell me."

"I don't..."

"You don't what?" Jordan continued to tug at her sexy top until her bare breasts were exposed and ready. He hovered over each erect nipple with no resistance; his breath was warm and his deep moans made her shake in anticipation.

"I don't...don't want you to stop." She begged him not to tease her this time. She explored his lap with a steady, circular rhythm, her thighs stabbed by the sword beneath her.

"Wait." He raised his head and stared into her lustful eyes.

"What's wrong?"

"Nothing's wrong. Everything is right." He brushed back her silky hair. "Do you have any idea how much I've missed you? Your smile, your laugh, that little pout on your face when you don't get what you want."

"Jordan." She hit his firm left pec and she laughed the way he remembered. "You're making me blush, you big teddy bear."

"When you left Timberton, nothing was the same. I wasn't the same. For the next two years, I woke up every morning wishing I could pick up the phone and call you just to hear your voice. I knew you needed a clean break, a fresh start. I didn't want to make things harder for you than they already were. With each day that went by, I forced myself to push aside all of the memories, the good and the bad. The pain of losing you ran so deep, I couldn't think of you at all. I had no choice but to forget us."

"Jordan, I'm so sorry." She kissed his lips as he spoke the last word. "I missed you too. Believe that."

"I want to believe it. I do believe it."

Their bond grew stronger, weakened only by the secret he held.

"You are one incredible girl, Madison Pike."

"Tell me more," she demanded, as if she knew there was a hidden truth.

"I want you, not just for now, but forever." He embraced her like an exotic flower with fragile petals. The thought of making love to Maddie consumed him, but the fear that she would cast him from her life for good once she found out the truth was a heavy burden. His unsavory relationship with her sister collided with the animal instinct to enter her, and he pulled away. The shame he felt for taking advantage of Michelle and using her to fulfill his sexual needs when Maddie turned him away so many years ago would be their ultimate demise unless he found a way to come clean, and soon.

Maddie held onto Jordan, reveling in him until she heard the voices of townies on an afternoon stroll; their chatter chilled the sweat that dripped off Jordan's brow onto her thigh.

"We'd better get going." She jumped off him and straightened up; she kept her disappointment a secret. A few buttons were missing from her shirt. She wasn't sure if they flew off in the heat of passion or if he ate them.

"You are mine," he said and gave her a gentle kiss on her cheek.

"Why, yes, sir. Whatever you say," she answered with a Southern drawl that turned him right back on.

"Wow, it's almost dinnertime." He put the car in reverse. "Why don't we see what Ally is up to? Maybe take her out. Show her around a little more."

"Yeah, a good idea."

"Poor girl has been shoved to the side with everything going on this week," Jordan said, ashamed of his lack of Southern hospitality.

"She's fine. She loves it here and is finding plenty of stuff to do, trust me."

"Oh, yeah?"

"Oh, yeah." She parroted him. "Haven't you heard the rainbow shower parties in the middle of the night? She loves hanging out at Willy Tucks Tavern with Timberton's finest cowboys and bet on who can ride the mechanical bull the longest. The winner and his friends end the night here. Sometimes it gets a little crazy."

"I guess I sleep through it. You special ladies are on the other side of the house, remember?"

"True that."

It didn't take long to get back to the ranch. Ally greeted them wearing a red bikini and one of the cowboys she'd met the night before. It was as if he was glued on.

"Hey, guys," she sputtered with a mouth full of beer.

"Hey." Maddie gave her the raised eyebrow. "You doing okay?'

"Oh, yeah." She pointed at the bare-naked hot guy that hid behind her with little success. "How'd it go today?"

"I'll fill you in later. You look a little busy." She pursed her lips; red lipstick covered only the edges of her mouth.

"Okay, cool. We'll be out by the pool if you want to come out and play with us."

"We might." She coughed and looked to the floor without one comment about her cowboy's low-hanging fruit.

"She looks like she doesn't need us to entertain her." Jordan hugged Maddie and pulled her close.

"Yup, she sure looks like she's doing just fine."

He went in for a slow kiss. She wrapped her arms around his neck, leaped over his belt buckle, and wrapped her long legs around his waist so he would have to carry her to the next room.

"Let's talk about everything tomorrow." She used his broad chest as her temporary resting place. "We'll have all day to go over things again. The storm could keep us inside all day."

"I'm going to look forward to that."

"Why don't you go grab us some beer? I'll go up-stairs, change and meet you outside. Let's join those two crazy kids by the pool."

"Sounds good to me."

Jordan grabbed two beers, some raw hamburger patties, and the delicious rolls Miss Camilla baked fresh that morning. He headed outside to the spar-kling, blue kidney-shaped pool with a rumbling wa-terfall where his friends mingled, and Judge and Jury dog-paddled up and down the center of the pool in unison. Everyone made themselves right at home. It was paradise.

"What do you say we fire up the grill?" he asked his oversexed houseguests who piled on top of each other. The giant, green frog float bounced across the clear water as Ally rode her cowboy with only a thong between them.

"We're in. Ally said as she stopped her award-win-ning ride just enough to answer and then went back to business just as fast.

Maddie walked out in her new emerald green thong bikini, courtesy of the one and only Jordan Kingston.

He couldn't take his eyes off her, a hazard when cooking over an open fire. Jordan managed to prepare dinner, but not without evidence of his distraction. The burgers were more than well done. Each patty was more fitting for a horse's shoe than for human consumption, but no one seemed to mind.

The foursome relaxed outdoors for the remainder of the evening and didn't go inside until the air changed. The weekend storm was on its way. Timberton's officials made the right call by moving the festival to Sunday this year.

Saturday came and went. Jordan and Maddie couldn't be more prepared. Since Roger was on their radar, their plan needed to be executed with precision so he wouldn't be tipped off. Taking him off guard would be just as important as cornering Colin.

She knew from her years of experience litigating all types of cases, their actions could be considered false imprisonment, but she was willing to take the risk if it meant she would find out the truth.

Sunday morning was finally here and the anticipation for the day was at a fever pitch. The sun was strong and bright at 7:00 a.m. with no signs of the storm that had descended on Timberton the day before. As soon as the rain let up during the night, the town's volunteers went to work using the moon and portable spotlights to finish setting up the festival rides, stages for the clown shows, food stands, and booths for the local craftsmen to show off their handiwork.

"You ready for this?" Jordan woke up in Maddie's room after a restless night's sleep.

"Let's do this." She jumped out of bed and dressed in no time flat. A pair of painted-on jeans, a white tank top, and hair in a bun was a look that took no time to complete. She looked like she did when she was a kid, and it was not by accident.

Ally and her hot boy toy helped Miss Camilla load up Jordan's SUV to transport her fine foods to the festival. Maddie pulled the convertible around and waited out front for Jordan. She put pressure on him to hurry so she would be wired up and ready to hit the ground running before the festival opened up at nine o'clock sharp. The wire was at the suggestion of the detective. It did not fit into her plan, but she complied to look like a team player.

"Jordan, you're worse than a woman. Hurry up!"

Another five minutes went by before he made it down to the car, too long for her liking. The second he shut the door to the racecar-worthy convertible, she sped off with the gas pedal to the floor.

The duo beat Miss Camilla's caravan of food to Timberton Park where the town traditions would take place. Soon the plush acres would swarm with townies and visitors alike. The entrance was as grand as it always was with a twenty-foot banner flying high above the entrance that welcomed anyone and everyone with open arms.

"Jordan, look." She pointed up to the massive canvas display that passed overhead as they drove under it.

Welcome to the Timberton Lake Festival written in bold black letters was like a hug, and the images with vibrant colors implied solidarity, unity, and acceptance. Maddie was in awe of her town's message and made her miss home more than ever.

The festival had grown in size over the years. More rides, more games, more booths. Its growth kept up with the population of Timberton that had multiplied tenfold since she'd left so many years ago. People came to the quaint town in droves, one of the reasons Kingston Enterprises planned to expand the park in the first place. Developing the land that used to carry the Old Timber Yard was the perfect way to give back to the community.

"Wow, this is really something." She looked around the park as if she'd never been there before.

"It's a good time. Everyone enjoys it. It still brings people together," he answered, already out of the car and past the headlights to open her door for her. On any other day, she'd be out of her seat before him, but today she wanted to take it all in before her focus shifted from Timberton's hometown girl to resident super sleuth.

Ten parking spots away, a white van disguised as a local news truck, complete with a receiving dish on the roof, awaited her arrival. This was the main hub for the operation, where she'd be fitted with a wire and where Jordan would remain to keep his eye on the detective in case he pulled a fast one.

Four knocks, each five seconds apart, signaled the men inside that she was here. An officer dressed in black slid the door open to let Jordan and Maddie step in. The van's ceiling was tall enough for most people to stand up straight, but Jordan's size required him to maintain an uncomfortable arch.

"Roger." Jordan nodded.

"Ready?" Roger offered his right hand for a friendly shake.

Jordan looked at his mitt for a moment before he responded.

"Yeah, all set." The hesitation didn't go unnoticed by the detective, but no comment followed.

"Okay, let's wire you up." Roger signaled to Officer Troy to handle the task.

"Hello, Ms. Pike," Officer Troy said. "Do I have your express consent to begin placing the wire on your person?"

"Yes, go ahead." She allowed him to lift her shirt a bit. Jordan watched to make sure she wasn't exposed more than necessary.

"Okay. As we discussed, we will have Officers Peterson, Smith, and Ellis out in the field with you, plain-clothed and ready to act upon your cue. Once you have him secluded in a remote area, get as much information as you can and get out of there. We'll be listening in and will act at the first sign of any trouble, but make sure you find an area where we can get to you easily," Roger said.

Jordan and Maddie glanced at each other before she answered.

"Okay, will do."

It wasn't long before she was ready to go. "Wish me luck," she said as she gave Jordan a peck on the cheek and made her way into the park to scope it out. There wasn't much time left before the nine o'clock hour arrived and the hordes of people gathered outside the perimeter would flood the grounds.

"Testing. Testing," she said as she walked through the booths to see if the tiny mechanical object could handle the task.

"We got you." Officer Troy sounded clear as a bell through her pea-sized earpiece.

"Peterson, check in." Officer Troy continued the roll call.

"Check," Peterson answered, followed by the same response from Smith and Ellis.

Everyone was in place.

Maddie found the perfect location to get Colin right where she wanted him, but she wasn't going to share it with her audio buddies.

The gates opened and people started to pour in. It was a perfect 85 degrees and the sun came out to play like everyone else in town. Almost instantly, Maddie was bombarded with good wishes and welcoming words from everyone who knew her and her family. There wasn't anyone in Timberton who didn't shop at Pike's Market at one time or another to pick up supplies or groceries.

Maddie's focus never wavered from her main purpose until an older woman got her ear.

"Well, hello there, Miss Madison," she said with a pronounced Southern drawl under a big, wide-brimmed hat shielding her from the sun. "I'll be damned. How have you been, dear? I heard you were in town."

"I'm doing well, Miss… I'm sorry, I apologize, I don't remember your name."

"I'm Miss Eloise Montgomery. A friend of your mama and daddy. You know, from the market and all," she said as she grabbed Maddie's hand and shook it like the wet laundry she hung outside to dry every weekend.

"Of course. Very nice to meet you." She returned the display of affection, careful not to impose the same amount of pressure to the old woman's arms.

For the next seven minutes, Eloise went on about all the happenings in the town of past and present. She seemed to know anything and everything about everyone. Most of what she said fell on deaf ears until she mentioned the Stones. Suddenly, Eloise became the princess of the ball.

"Miss Eloise, why don't we go over here in the shade for a while? I'd love to hear more." Maddie guided her to a bench under the giant oak tree. The officers who listened in couldn't help but let out some laughter at the idea Maddie had been unwillingly sidetracked by this nice old lady, but the detective remained silent. Jordan took note of the fact that Roger looked like someone just hit him in the face with a hammer. Roger excused himself and stepped outside, but could still hear the audio through his device.

"Oh, yes, that would be nice, dear. I have so much more to tell you." She grabbed her embroidered purse with both hands and walked at a quick pace for a woman just shy of her seventieth birthday.

The chatter was fluid and delivered without a pause. Gossip was obviously her passion.

"So what about the Stone family? Do you know them?" Maddie probed for more.

"Well, yes. I think I'm one of the few people in the world who does." She leaned in closer to Maddie with her hand up near her cheek to shield the next sentence from the public. "Crazy family. Abusive to the kids."

"Kids?" Maddie pressed her so she could assess whether Eloise was firing on all cylinders or a little crazy.

"Yes." Her voice increased by two octaves to emphasize her point. "Did you know that there were *two* kids in that crazy house? Not a lot of people know that. It was a big secret."

"Really?" She leaned in further to encourage Miss Eloise to keep going.

"Mm hmm," she said with a clenched mouth and a confident head nod. "Yup, two boys. Colin and Connor. Twins, you know."

"Twins?" Maddie reacted with some anger that took Eloise off guard.

"Are you okay, dear?" She backed out of their huddle.

"Oh, yes, of course. I'm sorry. I was just a bit surprised. Please, tell me more. This is so interesting." Maddie calmed herself and continued with a delicate inflection.

"Well…" Miss Eloise said thrilled to continue to share her stories with anyone who would take the time to listen. "The boys were big troublemakers.

Of course, you see, the father hit them all the time and the mother was so afraid of him. She never did anything about it. Until one day, when the boys turned four years old, the boy's uncle, Mrs. Stone's brother, got her out of town with Connor. She left Colin here with their father because she didn't think she could care for both of them, and the boys hated each other anyway. I think it was a mistake, if you ask me."

On that note, the detective interjected and announced he saw Colin entering the park.

Maddie was shocked at what Eloise just told her. One thing was for sure, Eloise Montgomery was in her right mind and she'd be sure to speak with her again.

"Miss Eloise, I have so enjoyed our conversation. Thank you for spending some time with me today." Maddie stood up and gave her a kiss on the hand. "If you'll excuse me, I have some business to tend to, but I would love to get together for tea soon. Would that be all right?"

"Oh, yes, dear. I will look forward to it. I have so much more to tell you."

"I am counting on it." She left her with a satisfied smile.

"I'm on my way." Maddie spoke into her device as she ran to the front gate to meet the others. "I'm here at the entrance. I don't see him."

"Okay, spread out. There's a lot of people here. He must already be lost in the crowd," the detective said.

Maddie hunted for him, but found the detective's timing strangely convenient. When Miss Eloise offered details, Roger reported he saw Colin come through the entrance and Colin was nowhere to be found.

"Jordan," she said into the device. "Are we on the same page?"

"Yes, same page." He let her know he felt the same way about Roger's timing without revealing himself to the others connected to the audio feed.

It had been hours since the so-called sighting. Colin hadn't been seen by anyone else.

The festivities were in full swing. Miss Camilla's booth had its customary string of people lined up to taste her special recipes. The bands played old time jazz, and the smell of charcoal burgers and fried chicken permeated the air. There was not one stuffed animal that hadn't been adopted by a child whose parents spent their hard-earned money on the carnival games just to bring a smile to their innocent faces and make the festival a happy tradition.

As the clock ticked away, Maddie continued to walk the grounds, checking in with the others to get an update. Just when she thought Colin would not show up, she caught a glimpse of him loitering around the food area.

"Jordan, I think I'd like to get something to eat. Can you meet me at the fried chicken stand?" Her request to get something to eat was the secret code to let him know that she spotted Colin and it was go time.

"Sure, be right there." With no one the wiser, Jordan headed over to the fried chicken stand.

"Hey." He came up behind her.

"Okay. Like we planned. Get him onto the Ferris wheel. I'll ambush him. He won't be able to get away," she said. "Go."

Jordan searched out one of the young women who took private riding lessons at the ranch. It wouldn't be hard to find a willing participant since almost every girl in town had taken lessons with him at one time or another, and most wanted to please the sexy cowboy.

Kimberly Johansson was the lucky girl in his line of sight this morning. Her father had rented out the arena for her twenty-first birthday and her infatuation with Jordan was no secret.

"Kimberly. Hey, there. Beautiful day." He turned on the charm and flashed an irresistible smile.

"Jordan. Hi." She placed her hand over her heart. "Yes, such a great day."

After more conversation and a few sincere compliments, he thought she was ready for the big question.

"Miss Kimberly, may I ask you a small favor?"

"Of course, anything for you," she answered, ready to do anything he asked.

"My friend over there is feeling a little down today. Would you mind asking him to take a ride on the Ferris wheel with you? It will boost his spirits, I'm sure."

He pointed to the person who stood alone by the arcade.

"Do you mean Colin?" Her eyebrows raised high enough to meet her pixie bangs.

"Yeah, but don't tell him I sent you over. It will be better if he thinks you asked him yourself."

"Sure. Yeah, okay." She agreed and traced her finger along the edge of his jaw line. "You know I'd do *anything* for you."

"Thanks, Kimberly. I owe you one."

"You bet you do." She walked away with the intention to cash in later in the day.

"Excuse me, Colin?"

"Yup." His face leaned almost parallel to the ground.

"I really want to go on the Ferris wheel over there, but I'm afraid to go alone. Would you please do a girl a favor and go up with me?"

"No, I don't think so."

Kimberly turned and looked at Jordan who stood out of Colin's line of sight and shrugged. He gave her a wink and a wave to encourage her not to give up.

"Please, Colin. I am dying to go up. Pretty please." She gave him the look of a damsel in distress.

"Well… Uh… Okay. I guess so." He agreed after an uncomfortable pause.

She grabbed his hand and the unlikely couple waited in line for the current passengers to disembark and the new set of passengers to be loaded on.

"It's almost our turn," she said.

"Yeah, almost."

New passengers boarded, and with just two seats remaining, the attendant waved them on.

Kimberly lifted the safety bar and sat down first. Colin followed behind, but not without trepidation.

"C'mon, Colin." She patted the open space next to her.

Just as Kimberly extended her arm to bring down the bar and close it, Jordan appeared from behind the crowd and reached for Kimberly's hand.

"Kimberly, can you come with me please?"

Kimberly and Colin look at each other, both clueless as to what was about to transpire. Before either of them could figure out what was happening, Kimberly was up and out of her seat and Maddie took her place.

Maddie secured the bar and hollered at the carnival attendant. "Move this thing. Now!"

Colin's face turned from pale white to fire engine red in a split second. As the Ferris wheel moved, Colin shook the safety bar to get out and he let out a string of grunts that sounded like the devil himself.

"Calm down, Colin. Relax." Her soft timbre diffused his rage. "Shh. Shh. It's okay."

"What the hell is going on?" Roger said into her earpiece.

"I think she has Colin cornered on the Ferris wheel, sir," Officer Troy answered.

"All men to the ride immediately!" Roger's panic was palatable. "Damn it. This is not what's supposed to happen."

Colin stared at Maddie. She looked and sounded just like Michelle. He seemed confused and paralyzed.

"Colin, I need you to tell me what you know about Michelle. Why do you have her necklace? Here, like this one." She lifted the pendant that lay on her chest and waved it front of him.

His face twitched and his aggression escalated once again.

"How did you get out?" His voice turned eerie and unfamiliar.

"What?"

"How. Did. You. Get. Out?"

"Out of where, Colin?"

"There is no way you could escape. How did you do it? How?"

Maddie picked up on what was happening. Somehow he thought she was Michelle. *Maybe it was a game they used to play as kids.* She wasn't prepared for this, but with her window of opportunity closing, she played along with his delusion.

"I just let myself out."

"That's impossible," he answered in a fit of rage. "You are not safe. Only I can protect you."

"I'm safe," she said.

Colin kept repeating himself. "You are not safe. You are not safe." He got more agitated every time he said it.

Jordan and the ground team could hear every word. Fearing for Maddie's life, Jordan ordered the attendant to get them down.

Colin acted crazier by the second. At the highest point in the air, he rocked the passenger car back and forth like a swing in a playground. The spectators below watched in horror as the bolts that held

the apparatus together ground against the metal
bars, causing them to weaken.

"Jordan!" She held on to the safety bar for dear
life.

"Hang on, baby!" he answered. "Help is on the
way. We'll get you down. Hang on."

"Colin, stop!" she said.

He was at the point of no return. Colin lifted the
safety bar and pushed Maddie out of the passenger
car.

"No!" Jordan stretched his arms into the empty
air as if he could reach her.

Maddie grabbed the old, frayed seat strap that
dangled out of the back of the car. She could barely able to hang on. Her arms were fully extended
and her legs flailed about like a rag doll. The worn
threads of the ancient strap snapped one by one; the
friction of the loose bolts gnawed at the edges of the
rest.

Parents covered their children's eyes and whisked
them away so they wouldn't see the inevitable. The
patrons' screams pierced through the once peaceful
bubble that surrounded the festival.

The passenger car made its descent toward the
ground as Maddie hung on for life.

"Pull yourself up!" Jordan was unsure if she could
still hear him through the device. "Swing your legs
and grab the bar with your feet!"

She couldn't gain control of her legs. With adrenaline running through her veins, she flung herself high enough clench Colin's right leg between hers and pulled as hard as she could.

"Here, you bastard!" She dragged him right off the seat.

He slid down her body and clutched her ankle in his hands; her body extended past its normal range. She blacked out for a few seconds from the searing pain and the spectator's screams of horror drowned out the background music that played throughout the festival's intercom.

"Hang on, you're almost down." Jordan begged her not to let go.

As soon as Jordan could reach a piece of Colin's flesh, he dragged him to the ground and placed a chokehold on him worthy of the Mixed Martial Arts highest honor. It took every officer at the festival to pull Jordan off him before he strangled him to death.

"I'm gonna kill you, you son of a bitch." He shook off each officer as if they were minor annoyances. "You're a dead man."

Meanwhile the first responders who arrived at the scene tended to Maddie. Brandon, her brother, was the lead firefighter on duty and ran to her aid.

"What the... What happened? Are you okay?" Brandon pushed her hair out of her face and examined her for injuries.

"I'm okay."

"Are you sure?"

"I think so. But my back…"

Jordan held her hand as Brandon and his team prepped her for transport to the hospital, then rolled her into the back of the ambulance. Brandon shut the double door behind them and tapped the van to alert the driver to move.

Officer Smith handcuffed Colin, read him his Miranda rights, and placed him under arrest for the attempted murder of Madison Pike.

Roger shook his head as Officer Smith and Ellis put him in the back of the cruiser, his face still blue from Jordan's vise grip.

Colin remained silent.

CHAPTER TEN

I t wasn't long before doctors released Maddie into Jordan's care with a recommendation to get plenty of rest for the next couple of weeks. Despite her emotional exhaustion, she was in good condition.

"Jordan, I want to stop by to see my mother," Maddie asked on the ride back to the ranch.

"Right now?" He thought this might not be the best time to take on the emotional gymnastics.

"Yes, I need to see her."

"Okay. If you're sure you're up for it." He turned the car around.

As Jordan pulled up in front of the lake house, Maddie could see her mother looking out the floor-to-ceiling window of their oversize chalet-style living room that overlooked the driveway. Quick as a scared mouse, her mother was out of sight.

"Where did she disappear to?"

"Do you want me to come in?"

"I'd like to go in alone, but will you wait for me? I won't be long."

"Of course. I'll take a walk around. Meet me down by the dock when you're done."

"Will do." She walked around to the driver's side of the convertible to give him a peck on the lips.

The front door was open, a sign her mother wanted her to enter. A good omen as far as Madison was concerned. She stepped in the spacious foyer, shut the door behind her, and looked around, hoping Mom had not changed her mind about spending time together and talking thing out.

One thing that did not change was the interior design of the house. She had forgotten how beautiful their home was and realized she hadn't appreciated nearly as much as she should have.

"Mom, are you up there?" Her voice carried up the wide circular staircase that led to the twenty-foot balcony and the upstairs bedrooms.

"I'm in the kitchen."

"Hey, are you okay?" She walked into the comfortable nook and gave her a hug. It was obvious

Brandon had not called her to tell her about the events of the day to spare her from more grief.

"Yes, I am glad you stopped by."

Her sentiment was music to Maddie's ears, one she had not been sure she would ever hear again.

They embraced for a long time without a word spoken. As far as Maddie was concerned, the message was clear: their relationship was on the mend. Now all it needed was time.

"Mom, you look a little pale," she asked as she caressed the side of her face.

"Mmm, I'm not feeling so well today."

"Maybe you should have gone to the festival? Get out a little bit."

"Your dad is at the market today and Brandon is working. Besides, I felt I needed to rest."

"It was actually a blessing you didn't go today," she answered under her breath.

"What, dear?"

"Oh, nothing. I was just saying I'd like to take a walk around the house."

"Well, let's head upstairs. I want to show you something."

Gail led her up the stairs, but was noticeably slow and weak. As they approached the last step, Maddie saw a photo of her and Michelle placed in the center of the mahogany credenza, a priceless family heirloom passed down from Gail's great-grandmother.

Maddie was more than a little surprised to see the photo. She assumed Mom had packed away everything that reminded her of them and buried it all amongst the dusty attic clutter.

Gail dragged her weary body to the end of the hallway and opened the door to Maddie's old bedroom.

"This room in the most precious room in the house, your dad used to say."

"Mom." Her jaw dropped as she walked in, overwhelmed by what she saw. "Everything is exactly the same in here. You didn't change a thing."

"You see, things were not as you thought they were all these years, my dear. I only dusted, mostly. I placed a few more things around the room from when you were very young to remind me of all the joy you brought to me your whole life."

Maddie walked around the room touching everything at least once. She inhaled the smell of the wood that just received a fresh coat of polish.

"You even kept my little sales log." Maddie picked up the small, spiral-bound notebook with worn edges that sat on the white, gold-trim end table at the side of the bed.

"Yes. You were precious. I will never forget how you went around the house collecting items for your pretend store. Remember how you'd set up a table in the living room with everything placed just so and Brandon would come by with the change from his piggy bank and buy everything you had for sale."

"I do remember. You went into Brandon's room after a few days, removed all the trinkets, and put them back in their proper place around the house." She flipped through the faded pages. "Look at this, Mom."

Maddie handed her the piece of cardboard that read, *"Sale. 1 cent. Please pay with a peny or a chek."*

"You were a little entrepreneur, but not a very good speller."

"I was always coming up with some idea or another." Maddie closed the notebook and placed it back as she found it so the room would remain undisturbed.

"Your father still sleeps in here sometimes. He misses you terribly. As do I." She sobbed and buried her face in her hands.

Maddie held her with a hug that would comfort the most wretched soul.

"Sit there for a minute." Her mom pointed to the edge of the bed that faced the lake. "You can see for miles and miles."

Tears welled up in Maddie's stunning blue eyes as she gazed over the calm waters.

"So many memories. Your father and I used to watch you girls play outside from this window. We would sit here for hours feeling blessed to have the most beautiful family in the entire world."

"Mom, I'm so sorry I took it all away from you."

"It was not your fault. It was for me to be strong for you, not you for me. I never should have let my grief and guilt come between us. I have wasted so much precious time. Precious time. And now..."

"We can start over. Let's fix this." Maddie embraced her.

"Madison, my dear. My time here is not long."

"What do you mean?"

"I am not well. I forbade your father or brother to tell you, but now you should know," she said. "My heart is very weak."

"What?"

"The doctors say my heart is riddled with disease. A transplant is my only option."

"What? Are they sure? Did you get a second, third and fourth opinion? I know some of the best doctors in the world. Come to New York with me. Let me help you."

"We'll see, but there is one thing you have to do for me before I die. Please."

"You're not going to die. Don't talk that way." She held her hand in hers.

"Find out what happened to Michelle. Please."

"I will, Mom. Believe me, I will."

Gail had used up every bit of energy she had left and could not continue to communicate very well. Maddie tucked her into her bed to rest and made sure she had some of her favorite sweet tea by her bedside. With a kiss on her forehead, she assured her they would talk about this more tomorrow.

"Jordan?" Maddie shouted of the back deck only twenty feet from the water's edge, hoping he was in earshot.

"Hey, down here." He hollered and waved to make sure she could see him amongst the trees.

Maddie ran down the steps two at a time to meet him and jumped into his arms.

"Hey, what's the matter, sweet thing?" He caught her in midair.

"Mom's very sick. Heart disease. She said the doctors told her she needs a transplant."

"I had no idea, babe. I'm so sorry to hear that." He caressed her back and then pulled her in close to comfort her.

"I offered to take her to New York and bring her see a doctor up there. I'm not going to lose hope, but I think she has. She said she only wants one thing before she dies and that is for me to find out what happened to Michelle. That's all."

"We will. Did you tell her that? We will," he answered with deep conviction.

"Yeah." She took Jordan's hand and pulled him down to sit on the warm sand with her.

The water reflected the light like a giant mirror and the tall, green, leafy trees lining the water's edge created a natural boundary that kept unwanted tourists from their private haven. Maddie made a promise to rest when she left the hospital, but her mother's plea fueled the fire in her belly. Not even her horrific ordeal could keep her down for very long.

"Jordan, I know we were going to wait to talk about what just happened, but I can't." She leaped with such force that she kicked a pile of sand into his lap. "Colin went nuts. He's crazy, we know that. But he snapped on a whole different level when he mistook me for Michelle. He kept asking me how I got out."

"Out of where?" Jordan asked as he brushed the sand from his crotch with one hand and blocked the glare of the sun with the other.

"I don't know. He also said that I, meaning Michelle, was not safe, assuming I got out of…where I don't know."

"It doesn't make any sense."

"I know. It doesn't. She's not with us anymore," she said.

"If Michelle's body didn't turn up, I might think the crazy bastard was holding her somewhere," Jordan said half joking.

His words resonated in her head. The lawyer in her took him seriously and made her start thinking outside the box.

"Wait. What if he is?"

"What?" Jordan looked at her as if she had four heads.

"What if he is holding her somewhere? What if he thought she *needed* protection and in his twisted mind, he locked her up to keep her safe?"

"Are you forgetting about one important fact?" he said, convinced she lost her mind or the medication she took was stronger than he thought. "Michelle's body was found."

"Was it? How do we know it was really her?"

"Okay, seriously?"

"Yes. How do we know? The body was so badly decomposed; the only thing we could see is that it was a girl about Michelle's age."

"Yeah, and that she was wearing Michelle's clothing."

"What if it was someone else who was wearing her clothes?"

"I don't know, Maddie. Sounds like a stretch to me," he answered. "And what about the DNA test? Roger said it came back with a positive ID."

Maddie looked at Jordan with pursed lips and squinted eyes and said, "Exactly. Roger. Roger said it."

He bought into her theory. "Do you think he ma-nipulated the results somehow?"

"Or just plain lied," she said. "I never saw the DNA report and I'll bet my dad didn't either. We all trusted him, but he's lying to us and I don't know why. What's he up to?"

"I don't know why either, but if he screwed around with the DNA results, his career would be over."

"Jordan, we have to get a look at that DNA test and we have to talk to Colin again."

"You can probably get your hands on the report easily enough, but talking to Colin is going to be damn near impossible. He is in the hospital, hand-cuffed to the bed, with police officers outside his doorway."

"That's true." She pursed her lips again. Her facial expression only proved her plan had already begun. She ran through scenarios in her head, cal-culating how, exactly, she would get it done. Defeat was never an option and difficult circumstances only made her work harder.

"He's under arrest for throwing you off the Ferris wheel. Remember?" He had to remind her that she'd had a pretty bad day.

"Shh." She waved her hand. "I'm thinking."

"Oh, boy. Here we go."

Maddie picked up her phone and placed a call to her high school friend, Katherine Quigley, who she reconnected with earlier that day at the festival. Good thing for Maddie, their small talk started with the exchange of cell phone numbers before catching up on the past nine years.

Just like many people in town who saw Maddie for the first time since she has been home, the two chitchatted about their lives, jobs, and relationships. Katherine offered her support and condolences, ending the conversation by asking her to call her if there was anything she could do. Little did she know Maddie would take her up on her offer sooner than she expected.

The name of Katherine's employer did not resonate with her until now. The fact that she works as a technician at KryHelon Labs, the same lab that conducted the DNA test per Roger's request, was music to her ears.

"Katherine, hey, it's Madison Pike." She signaled Jordan, excited to reach her on the first try.

"Hi, Madison, how are you doing?" she asked, taken by surprise. Katherine had just witnessed her hanging for dear life from a passenger car 135 feet in the air.

"I'm actually okay. Shaken up. But okay," she said with no pun intended.

"I'm so glad to hear you say that. Everyone was scared to death."

"Thank you. I appreciate everyone's concern."

"Madison, could you hold on for one second?" ·

"Of course."

A few minutes later Katherine returned and apologized for the distraction.

"So sorry about that. I'm at work tonight to catch up on some things so tomorrow morning isn't a total nightmare. Everyone is returning my calls all of a sudden. On a Sunday night. Figures, right?" She laughed at her own predicament.

"Oh, I won't keep you, but if you don't mind, could I bother you for a small favor?"

"Sure, no problem. What do you need?"

"Well, it has been a whirlwind since I've been back in town. The car accident for one thing, then the scare today."

"I can't even begin to imagine what you're going through," Katherine said.

"In all the commotion, I never got the chance to see the DNA report on my sister. The lawyer in me would feel better if I read it. Can you print me a copy?"

"I can certainly understand, but I'm really not supposed to release it without proper authorization, but let me do a quick search and see if I can view it for you."

"I don't want to put you in a—"

"Hold on," Katherine said, puzzled by her failed search attempt. "Give me second here. Something isn't right."

Madison had the patience of a newborn puppy. She listened to the sound of Katherine's fingers hitting the keyboard faster than an urgent message delivered in Morse code. Soon her finger stokes slowed, then stopped.

"It doesn't look like there is any report for Michelle Pike."

"What?" Madison straightened up, alerting Jordan something was wrong.

"No report. And I've cross-referenced it with the names of members of your family and nothing is coming up. This is so strange. I know that test was processed here."

"Could it be filed under something else?"

"No. Not typically. We index every case starting with the decedent's name. If no positive ID was obtained, it gets filed in a number of different ways, but that shouldn't be the case here."

"Strange." Maddie hit Jordan's thigh.

"I'm sorry, Maddie. I don't know why it's not coming up. Maybe you can ask Detective Hanoy. He gets a copy of all of all of these reports. I'm sure he has it."

"Okay, yes. I'll ask him. Thank you so much for your time. So good seeing you today."

"You too, Madison. Take care of yourself. And stay out of trouble."

"I'll try." She let out a faint laugh and stifled her reaction to what she had just learned. She hung up the phone and filled Jordan in. "No report. Nothing came up."

"You've got to be kidding me."

"Nope. Something is very wrong. And we are going to find out what it is."

"We?" He riled her up further.

"Yes. We."

"You're so sexy when you're mad."

"Listen, I have to go to the station tomorrow and you're going to come with me and distract Roger while I rummage through his things. See what I can find."

"Isn't that a little amateurish?"

"Keep it simple, stupid." She teased him with one of her playful punches.

He pinned her down on a sand patch and returned her flirtatious banter. She wiggled out of his grip and ran toward a small shed behind the majestic oak tree that cast an inviting shade and cooled its visitors.

"C'mon in here." She ducked her head a few inches to clear the opening of the doorway and exposed the red lace thong underneath the miniskirt she changed into.

"We need to talk." He leaned against the doorway and placed his arms on either side of the entrance, giving her no way out of the shed.

"We are talking, but fine. Let's talk here." She took off his hat and put in on top of her head before she hiked up her skirt to sit on the throw pillows piled on the floor. She scooted over to make a space for him. Even though the shed was big enough to fit a small dingy, there was just enough room for them to stretch out so she could show him how much she'd missed him and pick up where they left off the other day in the car.

"You are damn irresistible." He pushed back his thick, dark hair with both hands and lowered himself to take his place next to her. "I just want to—"

"You want to what?" She propelled herself on top of him. "Why don't you show me what you want?"

"Mmm, yeah." He resisted her advances. "We should talk."

"I want to be with you. Enough talking." She removed her tank top and placed his hand on her half-naked body. She urged him to explore her in every way.

The notion that he should tell her the truth, the whole truth, if they were to have any real chance did not escape him.

"I want to taste you." She licked her lips as she unlatched his belt buckle with her dainty hands and unzipped his fly one notch at a time. He had only a moment to stop her before there was no turning back.

"Do you like this?" She took him in her hand; the pleasure built up inside him with each skillful stroke.

"I...I can't let this go any further." He stopped her and held her close.

"I don't understand. Don't you want me?"

"Yes. More than anything." He lifted her chin and looked into her puzzled eyes. "Maddie, this is real for me. This is not some fly-by-night conquest. I know I have been reckless with women in the past, but I don't want to be *that* man anymore. I don't want to lose you. I want you to trust me."

"I do trust you, with my life."

He placed her head on his chest and kissed the top of her head. *If you only knew.* The guilt ate him from the inside out.

"You are my soul. My heart. My life." Jordan's breath was wet and heavy; his eyes welled up but she could not see them.

He had made love to Michelle in that shed, in that very spot. A betrayal tucked away in his mind, back to rob him of a life with the only woman he had ever truly loved.

"Let's go," he said, no longer able to sit within the four walls.

"Where?"

"I am going to take you to the finest restaurant in town." His abrupt end to their encounter raised doubt in her heart. "We'll stop by the ranch, shower, and put on our Sunday best."

He needed to free himself from the pine box that closed in on him like the lid of a coffin. There was no air, no escape. He was dead inside.

"Okay, if that's what you want." He was not himself and she knew it.

"Tomorrow, we'll get the answers you're after." He assured her he was on board with her plans.

With one final kiss, he led her straight to the car. For the first time since she had left so many years ago, he felt like he had something to lose.

CHAPTER ELEVEN

With no time to waste, Maddie separated the designer curtains made of fine fabric hanging in Jordan's bedroom. She felt the Monday morning sun encouraging her to own the day. Despite Maddie's chilling reintroduction to Timberton and this year's festival, she was no worse for wear. Most people would face a rough road to recovery, but she credited her martial arts training and some of her clients, who had been just as crazy as Colin, if not worse, for honing her remarkable coping skills.

"Get up, sleepyhead."

"Just a few more minutes." Jordan rolled over on his six-pack that she argued were more like eight.

"Do I have to pounce on you to get you going? C'mon, big boy." She mounted herself onto his inviting bare back with no mercy, causing his instant arousal. Her bounces got the blood flowing to all his muscles.

"Careful." He rolled over, providing no barrier to entry.

"Seriously, we have to get up. We have get down to the police station." She broke her straddle.

"What time is it?" He glanced at the clock she took from his nightstand to monitor the minutes as if she could make the clock tick faster. "Don't you think 7:00 a.m. is a little early?"

"No way." She sashayed her way into the shower. "Get your ass up."

Maddie had spent much of the night going over her mental road map. She fine-tuned every step of her plan so it would go off without a hitch. There was no time to explain the intricate details to Jordan before they arrived at the station; she'd just have to hope Jordan would be able to follow her lead as it unfolded.

"Good morning, Miss Pike, Mr. Kingston." Officer Troy greeted them and pointed to the two chairs in front of his desk. "Please, have a seat."

"Good morning." She observed only a few officers at their desks in the early hour. "Light staff today?"

"Everyone will start rolling in around nine o'clock," he answered as he pulled a pad of paper from the top drawer of his cold steel desk.

"What time do you expect Detective Hanoy?" she asked. "Aren't we meeting with him this morning?"

"I reckon he will be here a little late today," Officer Troy said. "He asked me to take this meeting. He is going to stop by the hospital to check on Mr. Stone and see if the doctors cleared him for questioning. I'd say he'll land here around ten-thirty or so, give or take."

"Detective Hanoy is going to question Colin this morning? Just him, alone?"

"Yes, Mr. Kingston. I believe so."

Jordan read Maddie's mind as if her thoughts were plastered in big, bold letters on her forehead.

"You know, Officer I'm not comfortable discussing what Colin did to me out here in the open." She waved her hand at the open area. "People walking by, interruptions, and distractions. What we need to discuss is rather personal. I'm sure you can understand."

Jordan saw right through her phony damsel in distress act and was impressed with her quick thinking.

"Understandable." He scanned the station to see if there was a suitable location available.

"There." Maddie pointed to the detective's locked office and gave the officer no chance to make any recommendations. "Let's go in there. I'm sure Roger wouldn't mind. He's a friend, you know."

Before the officer could object, she raced over to the door and waited for it to open as if it was a done deal.

"Okay, then," he answered. "I think it would be fine."

Jordan rose from his seat, gave the officer a neutral nod, and followed behind him as he fumbled with his keys.

"I know I have the right one on here somewhere." Officer Troy toggled through the keys for another few minutes, frustrated with the stack he accumulated. "I really have to do something about this someday."

Maddie played up her wounded soul act. She gained more sympathy from Officer Troy by the second.

"Don't worry, Miss Pike. We'll get through this as quickly as possible."

"Thank you." Her face slanted downward toward the floor, but she lifted her eyes to meet Jordan's as Officer Troy leaned over to try a different key.

"Ah. There we are. I knew it was here." It took five different keys before he found the winner. "I don't usually go into Roger's office when he's not here."

Officer Troy flipped the light switch and turned on the harsh, fluorescent lights that choked the room. It made the messy office seem more like an asylum than it already did.

"Have a seat," he said. "Is this better for you, Miss Pike?"

"Yes, much better, thank you," she answered while she scanned the room and assessed what she would rummage through first.

The officer questioned her for fifteen minutes before she gave Jordan a look that implied he should come up with something to distract him and give her a chance to make her move. Because this phase of her plan required some improvisation on Jordan's part, she had no idea what he'd do.

"Will you please excuse me for a minute?" Jordan stepped outside to make a phone call.

"Sure, Mr. Kingston," Officer Troy answered, unaware that he was about to be played.

Ten more minutes passed when a man in blue bolted into Roger's office informing Officer Troy a report just came in for a code 10-31, crime in progress at 2475 Berry Pine Lane.

"What?"

"You'd better hurry," his fellow cop said.

"Sorry, ma'am. If you'll excuse me. We will have to continue this a later date." He ran out the door, leaving her alone in the detective's office, a violation of the station's policies and procedures.

She suspected Jordan was behind the call, but unbeknownst to her, 2475 Berry Pine Lane was Officer Troy's private residence.

She made sure the coast was clear before she sifted through the papers piled high on Roger's desk and rummaged through the folders in his filing cabinet to see if she could locate the DNA report. There was no guarantee it would be in his office, but knowing the detective, he'd surely keep it close by.

Too frustrated by technology, Roger was as old school as they come. Metal filing cabinets filled to the brim, manila files, ballpoint pens and white lined paper were his friends. He was one of the few people on the planet who still handwrote letters, bought stamps, and mailed them at the post office. If the report was in his office, Maddie would find it.

"Can I get you some coffee while you wait for Officer Troy?" a young girl who interned at the station asked as she passed Roger's office on her way to the copy machine.

"I'm fine, thank you. I'll just hang here until the officer returns."

Maddie tackled the folders on his desk first. His organizational skills made the playroom of a two-year-old look neat and tidy. With no success, she targeted the beige steel filing cabinet that stood five feet tall, four drawers wide and lived alone in the far corner of his office.

The unsecured drawers were easy to open. She rifled through the blue folders looking for labels with a clue. One caught her eye almost immediately, the name CONNOR handwritten on the middle tab in pencil. If Miss Eloise had not mentioned Connor at the festival, Maddie might not have paid it any mind.

What do we have here?

Before opening it, she glanced down at her gold watch to check the time. The nine o'clock hour was fast approaching and soon the station would be crawling with cops.

"Time to go." She folded the blue file folder in half and stuffed it inside her expensive designer purse, a little bit of New York she'd brought with her.

Jordan waited in the car, anxious to know if their improvisation proved to be a success or failed miserably like a comic that had a bad set. The look on Maddie's face as she bolted out of the front door was proof enough for him.

"This crazy, long shot thing we just pulled off worked, didn't it?" he said with sarcasm.

"I think so." She removed the blue folder from its hiding place and handed it to him as if she'd gotten the last cookie in the cookie jar. "We can thank Miss Eloise for it."

He took the folder and placed it in the back seat of his car. "Do me favor, don't look inside until we get back to the ranch. You remember what happened the last time you looked inside something for clues while we were driving?"

"Ha, ha. Actually, I don't really remember much of it." She did not appreciate his humor, but admitted he did have a point.

Jordan didn't make it past the iron gates before Maddie had the infamous folder open.

"There's a lot of paperwork in here. Let's go in and spread it out on the table."

"You just can't wait, can you?"

"Nope, I didn't get that gene."

Jordan and Maddie opened the front door to find Miss Camilla deep into her breakfast ritual. The smell of coffee and her delicious cinnamon buns permeated the air. Ally bounced down the stairs with Cowboy Number Two as soon as the maple bacon hit the table. Her buff cowboys could eat a herd of cattle and this one appeared to be no exception.

"Good morning, my BFF." She walked on her tippy-toes to give Maddie a bear hug.

"Morning, ma'am." Her cowboy du jour wore not much more than a cowboy hat and a pair of familiar boxer briefs. The "JK" on the waistband was the first clue the undies lived in Jordan's dresser drawer.

"He doesn't go anywhere without his hat," Ally said with a giggle. "His jeans are in the wash."

As much as Maddie wanted to show interest in her friend's latest romp, her focus remained on her new intel.

"Whatchya got there?" Ally pointed to the layers of papers that suffocated the table.

"We are going to find out right now." Maddie took a small sip of the aromatic coffee so she would not burn her tongue and deprive herself of the full flavor of Miss Camilla's cinnamon buns on the first bite.

Healthy banter filled the room and the day looked promising. Paper after paper offered clues as to who Connor was.

"This guy is a mess. He has a rap sheet a mile long," Maddie said.

"What did he do?" Ally and Jordan answered in unison and read each other's mind.

"Almost all his arrests are for violent crimes of one kind or another."

"Did he spend any time in jail?" Jordan asked.

"Yes, quite a bit. He's been in and out of jail his whole life. The more serious crimes started when he was around seventeen and it escalates from there. Any more arrests and this guy is going away for a long time. I don't know how he got away with some of this stuff."

"What does he have to do with Michelle?" Ally asked.

"Let me see here." She turned page after page. "The only connection I see is that Connor is Colin's brother who I didn't know existed before Miss Eloise told me about him at the festival."

"That dude has a brother?" Ally said.

"Yeah, apparently. The Stone family was very secluded. No one really knew a lot about them."

"But didn't he go to school with you like Colin did?"

"No, he didn't." Maddie pointed to a section that showed relevant dates and past addresses. "It looks like he moved to Georgia with his mother, Zoe Stone, when he was four. It says here that when the Stones divorced the mother was awarded sole custody of Connor and the boys were separated."

"That's odd, isn't it," Ally said. "Separating young kids like that?"

"Yes, it is, but it looks like the judge determined it was in the best interest of the children for them to live apart. What's in their best interest is a judge's biggest concern when making these kinds of decision. It's the legal standard, and from what I see here, the boys were going to kill each other."

"Good thing you're a lawyer. I could never under-stand all that stuff." Ally stuffed a miniature cinnamon bun in her mouth, kissed her cowboy, and wiped the sugary glaze from the side of his lip that she left behind.

Maddie just flashed Ally a smile and kept on reading. "Wait a minute." She sat up in her chair as if she'd just come across a winning lottery ticket. "Could this be true?"

"What?" The whole table stopped in mid chew.

"Zoe Stone's maiden name."

"What is it?" The table mumbled with their mouths full.

She looked up at Jordan in a daze. "It's Hanoy. Her maiden name is Zoe Hanoy."

"What?" Jordan choked on his pastry.

"It looks like Zoe is Roger's sister. Colin and Connor are Roger's nephews," Maddie said as she digested this fact about as well as she digested the marbles she'd swallowed as a kid.

"That two-faced son of a...if there weren't la-dies at this table I'd..." Jordan's temper flared at his friend's betrayal. "You were almost killed."

"Okay, Jordan. Calm down." Maddie walked over to him and rubbed his back in an effort to diffuse his anger.

"I'm going to wreck that son of a bitch." He slammed his hand on the table, unable to hold back any longer. "I knew something was up, but I never expected anything like this."

"There's more," Maddie said.

She walked back to her chair and picked up the next round of documents that exposed Roger's betrayal even further. As painful as it was to hear, she had to get it all out.

"What is it?" Jordan said.

This was the angriest Maddie had seen him. Flashbacks of Richard's bad temper and the night he almost slapped her across the face in their New York apartment swirled around in her head, but she pushed the images away and continued.

"This report states that on the day of Michelle's disappearance, an Officer Bowman responded to a disturbance call at the Old Timber Yard at 1700 hours. That's around five in the evening. Michelle left us a couple hours earlier."

"And…" Jordan hung onto every word.

"The report states there were loud noises, screaming, and shouting coming from the yard. When the officer went in to investigate, he found four people in a heated argument. Two males who identified themselves as Colin and Connor Stone and two females who identified themselves as Michelle Pike and Sophia Johnson."

"But we looked there," Jordan said.

"Apparently, they were in the far corner of the yard. The secluded area. We wouldn't have thought to look there. It was dark and infested with who knows what, and there were piles of wood from old building projects, riddled with rusty nails and other dangerous things. We only checked the usual places we all used to hang out, remember?"

"What else does it say?" Ally asked.

"The officer told them to break it up and he let them go with a written warning."

"So Roger knew about this. There it is in black and white, in *his* filing cabinet." Jordan turned a new shade of red. "What about the DNA report?"

"No. Nothing on that."

"We have to talk to Roger. Now."

On his last word, the doorbell rang and no one moved. Miss Camilla walked by the dining room table to answer the door. As she wiped her hands on her flour-covered apron, she gave the entire a table a curious look, unaware of what caused the angst in the room. Her sharpest knife could not have cut through the uneasiness.

"I'll get it, Mr. Jordan," she said, her feet moved at a quick pace.

"Hello, Miss Camilla."

"Oh, Miss Eliza. Good morning. How are you?" She greeted her with a warm welcome, not sure if she should allow her all the way in the house without asking Jordan first.

"I've been better. Is Jordan home? I looked for him at the office, but the new girl at the front desk said he hasn't been in."

"Ah, yes. Good. Wait here please. I'll get him for you."

"Thank you," Eliza stepped into the grand hallway and waited as she was told.

"What are you doing here?" Jordan grabbed her arm and pulled her aside.

"I want to talk to you, please. I regret what I said to you. I want to make this right," she said while Jordan dragged her farther away from the dining room.

"Not now." He pressed his brow with his fingers to relieve the shooting pain that just pierced his skull.

"Jordan, who is—" Maddie asked as she walked to the door thinking it might be Roger, and if it was, she'd better intervene before Jordan puts his face through the stained glass window. "Eliza?'

"Madison." Eliza answered, less than pleased to see her looking so well.

"Eliza was just leaving." Jordan guided Eliza out the door.

"Jordan, I—"

The large, wrought iron K that hung on the front door nearly took her nose off when Jordan slammed the door behind her. A faint voice could be heard from the other side. "You're going to regret this, Jordan!"

"You probably didn't need to do that," Maddie said. She felt a little sorry for her arch nemesis.

"I don't have time for her."

"You still haven't told me the details of why you ended it with her, you know."

"Don't worry about that right now." He headed back toward the kitchen to get some water and cool down.

"I'm going to go to the hospital and confront Roger about what we know." She raised her voice so he could hear her over the noise of the ice machine.

"I'm going with you." He took a herculean gulp of his drink.

"No. I think you should stay here and let me handle this. You are too worked up and you are going to do or say something you will regret. Then I'll have to get you out of jail."

He took a deep breath and placed his glass of water on the counter.

"Fine." Jordan was reluctant to agree, but he knew she was right. "Call me the minute you know something."

"I will. I promise."

Maddie took her fancy purse and the keys to the convertible and made her way to the hospital. She vowed not leave there without getting into Colin's room, one way or another.

CHAPTER TWELVE

Maddie wasn't shy about using her charm and good looks to get information out of the handsome young resident assigned to care for Colin. Luckily for her, he didn't care about formal protocol. It only took minutes for the resident to divulge Colin's room number, his condition, and when he'd be moved from his room for tests.

In an effort to understand what Colin was thinking and how to manipulate him to giving up information she could use, she pressed her new friend a little harder and convinced him to show her his medical records.

"Colin suffers from a condition called erotomania. It causes him to have delusions." The intern pointed to the area in the report that discussed his diagnosis in detail. The report concluded that Colin believed he was in an ongoing relationship with Michelle Pike.

"Thank you…Isaac, is it?" She glanced at his badge. "You are very helpful."

"Anytime."

I have to call Jordan right away.

"Jordan," she said as she walked down the hallway to find a secluded area.

"What do you have?"

"I think Michelle could still be alive."

"What— Really? Are you sure?"

"No, but Colin's medical report says he thinks he is in a relationship with Michelle right now and he kept talking to me on the Ferris wheel in the present. Asking me how I got out. I have a feeling it is not just his imagination in play here."

"Is Roger there?"

"I haven't seen him yet. I don't know for sure."

"Be careful. Handcuffs or no handcuffs, Colin is a dangerous guy."

"I will. I'll call you back." She hung up the phone without waiting for a reply.

The nurse's station was bombarded with patients' call buttons going off at every turn. There wasn't enough staff to handle the volume, and Maddie knew that would work to her advantage. Dressed in a modest pair of dress pants and a white button-down blouse, she flew under the radar. But even in the most conservative of outfits, she was hard pressed to go unnoticed.

She planted herself about twenty feet away from Colin's room in a small alcove where she could assess the situation and calculate her next move. The two cops stationed right outside his room took turns leaving their post to take breaks, and there was still no sign of Roger.

"Isaac." She stopped her young, handsome intern as he walked by.

"Hi there."

"Could I ask you one more thing?"

"Of course. Anything. And I mean *anything*."

"How long have those guards been in front of his room?"

"There's been a cop or two standing there since the patient was brought in. I heard there will be two new guards taking the night shift." He checked his watch. "I expect them around five or so."

"Thank you. That is very helpful."

"Say, ah, if you have some time later, do you want to grab a bite to eat? My shift is over at four."

"Oh, you know, I would like to, but I have so much to get done on this case and time is running out. You understand how it is."

"Another time then?"

"Yes, of course." She said yes and shook her head no.

Maddie waited in the cold alcove for another half an hour before she called Jordan and updated him on her next move. He insisted she check in often or his deal to let her handle this part alone would end.

She stepped into the crowded elevator headed for the lobby. The cafeteria on the first level seemed like the only place to gain some privacy.

It stopped at every floor. People packed in like sardines, leaving little space to stand without getting to know their neighbor more than anyone wanted to. The men who rubbed against her never saw fit to apologize.

With one more floor to go, the elevator door opened and in walked Roger. He looked as worried as a guilty defendant. Despite the passengers' incredulous behavior, she welcomed their bodies as shields so Roger would not get a glimpse of her.

Roger took a step forward and he was off the ride. Last one on, first one off. He dashed toward the parking lot as if he had no physical impediment.

I wonder if he knows I'm here somehow. Maddie dialed Jordan's number to give him the news.

"The guards are changing shift at 5:00 p.m." She started right in without even giving him so much as a hello.

"What are you gonna do?"

"I'm going to sneak in. Maybe find a white coat and pretend I'm a doctor."

"Uh, just be careful. You're going to get yourself arrested if you're caught."

"I got this. Call you later."

The five o'clock hour fast approached. Maddie roamed the floors looking for a way to get her hands on a white coat. In a remote hallway that led to the third floor stairs, she observed one hanging over the back of a chair near a linen closet.

Hmm. I wonder if I could grab it without anyone seeing me? She placed an ear to the door. A table banging against the wall and simultaneous grunts told the whole story. *I'd venture to bet you won't miss your coat, whoever you are.*

The pocket held a stethoscope and a badge with the name of a female doctor.

It read, "Ellen Walton. Specialist/Reproductive Endocrinology."

Not quite the right field of medicine for Colin's issues, but this will have to do. She did not look anything like this Dr. Walton, but the photo was small enough to mask details and with any luck, no one would look close enough to notice.

"Good evening Dr. Walton," The newly minted guard said as he looked down at her phony badge.

"Good evening. I'll only be a minute," she said without direct eye contact.

"Wait, ma'am. Could I see your badge?"

Oh, shit. I knew that was too easy.

The guard held it in his hand and looked her up and down. He squinted to make out the detail in the substandard photo.

"I'm sorry ma'am. Could you please step over here for a moment?"

I'm screwed.

He stepped out of earshot, but watched her like a hawk to make sure she did not move. Maddie could see him talking into his shoulder mic, but she could not make out his words.

"If I could just explain," she said when he returned.

"No, ma'am. Please just wait here. Detective Hanoy is on his way."

"Oh, great," she said loud enough for him to hear.

"Sorry?"

"Nothing. Never mind."

Five valuable minutes went by before Roger limped around the corner.

He must have been on his way back here, or maybe he never left.

Their eyes locked like heat-seeking missiles. The unspoken words were louder than any voice could be, each knowing they were caught, but for different reasons.

"What's going on here, officer?" The detective pulled up his trousers.

"This woman attempted to enter the suspect's room under false pretenses."

"I see," he said. "I'll take care of this, officer. You can go take a break."

"I'm good, sir. I just arrived."

"Officer, I insist. Go."

"Very well, sir."

"Roger, what the hell have you done?" Maddie started in on him with no mercy.

"So you know. You know I'm Colin's uncle?" He stood with both hands on his hips.

"Yes. Damn right, I know. I know everything. I also know about Connor too, damn it."

"Nobody knows about Connor."

"Well, somebody does because this person was more than happy to tell me about him and I haven't been here in nine years," she said in a strong whisper so the argument would not be overheard.

"Okay, what do you want me to say?"

"What do I want you to say?" Her tone grew harsh. "I want you to tell me everything you know, and I mean everything. Then you are going to help me find Michelle. She is still alive, isn't she? Am I right?"

"I don't know. She might be."

"She might be? How could you do this to us? How? We trusted you." Her face came within inches of his.

"I'll tell you everything I know. C'mon, let's go somewhere private."

"No. You are going to tell me right here. I'm not leaving until I get the answers I came for."

"Fine. Okay, at least step over here." He pointed to a secluded area at the end of the hallway.

"You don't deserve to ask me to do anything, you bastard."

"I know you are upset."

"Upset! I want to stab you in the heart with the sharpest surgical tool in this place. Upset doesn't begin to describe it."

"I know. Please. Sit." He could not calm her down.

"You'd better tell me everything you know, and I mean fast."

Roger stood while Maddie leaned her backside against the window as if she was about to take a bullet.

"As you now know…" He stalled, afraid Maddie would spring forward like a lioness when he divulged the truth. "There was a disturbance at The Old Timber Yard the day your sister went missing."

"Yes."

"Colin came to me later that night. He was scared, delusional, and incoherent. At first I wasn't sure if he was just telling stories or if it all really happened."

"Can you please just get to the point?"

"He said that he went to the Old Timber Yard to be alone with Michelle. He loved her very much in his own way. His twin brother Connor had come back to town for a few days. Running from the law, as usual. He was with his girlfriend at the time, Sophia Johnson. A girl he met in rehab with no family to speak of. Connor took Sophia to the Old Timber Yard to party and found Colin and Michelle sitting on top of a stack of wood in a secluded part of the yard. Colin said they were just talking. Not bothering anybody."

The news was almost too much for Maddie to hear, but she managed to dredge up a response. "Your nephew has been in a lot of serious trouble by the looks of his rap sheet."

"He's trouble. No doubt about it. My sister and those two boys suffered a lot of abuse. By the time the boys were four years old, they'd suffered a lifetime of terror."

Despite the abhorrent circumstances, Maddie found herself feeling sorry for the kids.

"Connor and Colin fought to the death almost nearly every time they entered the same room. Connor taunted Colin and knew his triggers. He would get Colin to the point of no return. Rage personified."

"I experienced some of that rage. His demeanor changed on the Ferris wheel in a split second," she said.

"Yes, and that evening was no different. According to Colin, Connor started in on him like he always did, but this time he went after Michelle too."

"What?"

"Connor attacked her. He put his hands around her neck and threw her to the ground." Roger hesitated and bowed his head.

"What?" Maddie said again, but this time she stepped toward him so he was forced to look into her eyes while he finished the story.

Roger let out a big, breathy sigh before he was able to continue.

"He ripped off her clothes and tried to rape her." Roger feared Maddie would make good on her threat to stab him right in the hallway.

She slapped him in the face as hard as she could. An instant wave of nausea came over her. All she could think about was how scared Michelle must have been, and as far as she was concerned, it was all her fault.

"Do you want to hear the rest?" His tone warned her that it wasn't going to get any easier.

"I want to hear it all. Don't you dare hold anything back. If I find out you did, you will not live to see another day. Do you hear me?"

"Understood." He knew her threat was real.

"Go on."

"Colin saved her. He took a tire iron from a pile of rusty tools, swung it as hard as he could and hit Connor on the back of the neck, causing him to fly off her and go after him again. Colin was no physical match for Connor's strength."

"Colin saved her?"

"Yes, Michelle was everything to him. That I know for sure."

"Go on." She paced the floor with small pivots to change direction.

"Sophia went to Michelle's aid. She stood her up and gave her the clothes off her back since Michelle's clothes were ripped to shreds and she was nearly naked. The boys were viciously attacking each other at that point. The hate and anger that built up between them over their lifetime all came out on that day. One of them wasn't going to make it out of there alive. Connor put Colin in a chokehold and ready to break his neck when Michelle ran toward them and jumped on Connor's back, forcing him to let go."

"What?" Maddie was unable to hold back the tears any longer.

"Connor released his grip on him and shoved Colin with brute force right into Sophia. They fell onto the pile of rusty tools with Colin landing on top of her. He could not pull her up. She wouldn't budge and blood poured out of her mouth. A sharp, metal spike that stuck straight up in the air pierced her back and she died instantly."

"I can't believe this." She cupped her mouth in disbelief. Roger stepped away from her as he concluded the facts.

"Connor forced Colin to dress Sophia's body in Michelle's ripped clothing, dig a grave where they stood and bury her on the spot. Michelle was also forced to help, but was physically unharmed. The only insurance Connor felt he had against Colin ratting him out was to take the only thing he cared about in the world - Michelle. He threatened to kill her if he told anyone. He knew if he were caught, he'd get the chair. With his criminal history, no one would ever believe it was an accident."

"So she is still alive? Tell me she is still alive. Please."

"I don't know for sure, but based on the note Connor sent to Colin, it looks like there's a chance."

"What note?"

"Connor is serving a seven-year sentence in a maximum security prison for drug trafficking and attempted murder. He's got six months left. While doing his time, he became very religious. He changed. He wanted to make things right. A year ago he sent letters to everyone he could asking them to forgive him for all the pain he caused them during his life. He even wrote a letter to a small shopkeeper he stole from and brutally assaulted."

"He's been in nearly seven years? Where has Michelle been with for the past seven years? Where is she?" The thought made her sicker with every word, but she had no choice but to continue delve deeper into the possibilities.

"Connor got involved with a criminal organization, a bad group of people. These guys are *really* bad news. Drugs, human trafficking, you name it.

"Roger, what are you saying?"

"Michelle lived on the leader's compound, according to his letter to Colin. When Connor became one of the organization's most valuable and trusted leaders, he got involved in deals that were more nefarious and got caught in a sting operation, but never gave up any names. He remained loyal to the organization, and in exchange for his loyalty, Connor called in a favor and arranged it so Colin could go see Michelle. The deal was that once Colin arrived at the compound he'd be filled in on the rest, but he never divulged what *the rest* was. I never could find out."

"You son of bitch!" She pulled on the lapel of his ragged, brown jacket with both hands ready to slay him. "Where is she? Tell me now!"

"She might still be at the compound, but I don't know." He pried himself loose from her vise grip. "I saw the letter lying out in the open in Colin's room one day when I went to the shack to check on him. His father, Ely, left the shack a few years prior, and Colin became more of a recluse than ever before. I confronted him about the letter and that's when he told me he went to see her. She was there a year ago, but who knows now. Colin won't say a word."

"Why didn't you get her out of there when you found out where she was?" She showed Roger no mercy. "Why didn't you do the right thing, damn you! She could still be alive out there. Suffering, abused, alone, scared! And why did you let us think Michelle was the one dug up? Why?"

"I had to protect the boys. When they dug up the body, everyone thought it was Michelle because of the clothing, but the DNA proved it wasn't her. I had the DNA results altered. Then I had the report deleted from the lab database."

"You are going down for this, you pathetic, sorry excuse for a human being. Waste of flesh is what you are. But first you are going to take me to her. Do you understand me? Do you? Answer me?" She pushed him flat up against the wall and stared into his lying eyes like she was possessed.

"Yes." All his blood rushed to his head; his bad leg collapsed under him. "I'll take you."

"Don't move one inch," she said as she pointed her finger within centimeters of his runny nose.

She dialed Jordan with one press of a button. "Meet me at the hospital right away. The good detective has something he needs to show us."

"On my way."

CHAPTER THIRTEEN

Maddie escorted Roger down the elevator as if he were under arrest, an event she would bring about.

"Jordan will be here any minute… detective." She used his title with no respect. "Do you know how to get to this compound?"

"Yes, it's about a one-hour drive north of here."

"You'd better hope she's okay, that's all I'm going to say to you." She clutched his right arm with a tight grip.

The bored-out motor of Jordan's sports car announced his arrival. He pulled up to the hospital entrance and skidded to a complete stop.

Maddie opened the rear door, placed her hand on his head to lower him into the seat, and sat in the back with Roger so that she could keep an eye on him. Jordan would kill him with his bare hands if he knew what she'd just learned.

The car ride was hostile. Jordan's use of profanity was worthy of a deep cleanse. There wasn't enough soap in Timberton to wash away the grit.

It took approximately one hour to arrive, just as Roger said. The roads were narrow and dark. It was as if civilization just vanished. No trees. No structures. No people.

How could it be this close, yet so barren? Where is he taking us?

The later hour and the darkening sky gave them an edge. Roger told Jordan to approach the compound with caution and not get too close. It was clear that he had been here before.

"Park there." Roger pointed to a space overrun with brush. "We won't be detected if we plant ourselves here."

Cement blocks barricaded the front entrance. The thirty-foot-high sheet metal and barbed wire barrier hid the heinous crimes that took place within the perimeter. Evil consumed the air around the fortress, and the metal spikes that protruded from the fence's highest point threatened to tear the flesh off the bones of anyone who dared to challenge it.

"How did Colin get into see her?" She forced the detective to reveal more information.

"I don't know. He wouldn't tell me. He just said he came to see her. I swear it." His declaration was meaningless. If she wanted to know the truth, she'd have to find out for herself.

"How are we going to get in?" Jordan scanned the grounds and analyzed the impermeable, bullet-proof barrier.

"Jordan, you stay here with *him*," she said, unable to speak his name. "I'm going to find a way in and take a look around. I'm small. I'll find a spot to break in. The metal barrier doesn't look like it goes all the way around, see?" She pointed to a stretch of fence around the bend that looked like wood.

"It's too dangerous. I can't let you do that," Jordan said.

"You have no choice. I'm doing it."

"Damn it, Maddie! Will you just stop and think this through before you go and get yourself killed?"

"Roger, give me your gun. Now." She brushed off Jordan's comment and turned to Roger with her arm extended. If he didn't want to spend his final years in a cold jail cell, he had no choice but to comply with anything she asked.

He pulled his 9mm semiautomatic pistol from his waistband holster and handed it to her before she ripped it from his waist.

"Now give me the one around your ankle." She held out her free hand.

He leaned down and unstrapped the .40 caliber gun he kept hidden.

Jordan just rubbed his head, more out of fear for her safety than surprise at her gumption.

"Don't you think we should call for backup?" Jordan made one more attempt to talk some sense into her.

"No way. These thugs are watching for cops. I have to do this my way."

Without another word, she hid one handgun behind her back lodged between her bare skin and the waistband of her pants, and headed to the far end of the compound where the fence turned from steel to wood.

The half-inch spaces between the wooden slats provided a clear view into the lit interior of single-level row houses not far from the perimeter. Children played on the dry, brown grass right outside their front doors. Torn, discolored bed sheets connected forts made of old cardboard boxes and children's small faces peeked through worn tires used to make an obstacle course.

What is this? It looks like a little neighborhood.

She walked with a low profile around to what seemed like the back of the row houses, gun cocked and ready. As she took a step closer to the wooden fence to peek through the slats, her foot kicked a hard tin object that bounced against a stack of rocks. Her body stiffened for fear the noise gave her away, not one muscle in motion and not a breath exhaled. Once she felt invisible again, she crouched down to take a better look.

She leaned in as close as she could, her jaw flush against the splintered wall.

"Oh, shit." She fell backward onto her hand with the gun still cocked.

She pulled herself up and resumed her spot against the fence. A tiny eyeball looked at her from the other side. Her instincts told her there was no threat and her gut was usually right.

"Hi." Her tone was soft and gentle. "What's your name?"

"I'm Tommy."

"Hi, Tommy, my name is Maddie. Nice to meet you."

"Nice to meet you." He imitated her.

"How old are you?"

"I'm five. I can read now." He stood straight up, proud of his grown up accomplishment. She could no longer see his tiny eyeball.

"That's great, sweetheart. You are such a big boy."

"Yeah. That's what my mommy says."

"Is your mom in that house right over there with the big brown flower pot on the front step?"

"Yup. That's my house. And that's my room," He pointed in a random direction.

"Do you have lots of friends here?"

"No, not too many. Everyone is old."

"Old? Not too many kids to play with?"

"No. Just some."

"Do you have any brothers or sisters?"

"Yes. I have one sister. She's annoying."

"Tommy?" A woman's voice called from the porch. "Time to come in now. Where are you?"

"Over here, mommy." He turned his back to face the sound.

Maddie retrieved the gun and assumed combat position just in case this exchange was about to go bad, although something told her this woman was not the enemy.

"Darling, what are you doing over there?" She walked toward him to see what her little angel was up to.

"There's a nice lady right there."

Not sure whether to be frightened or laugh at her son's assertion, she knelt to peek through the ever-popular slat. "Is anybody there?" she asked with a slight tremble in her voice.

Maddie chose to roll the dice and go all in. "Yes, miss. My name is Maddie. I am a friend."

"Huh—oh my goodness!" She cupped her mouth to stifle herself.

"I'm here to find my sister." Maddie gambled with full disclosure. This might be her only chance to find out what was going on behind the wall.

"Your sister?" She engaged in conversation with no hesitation.

"Yes. My sister, Michelle, was taken to this…I guess you call it a compound, many years ago. I'm looking for her. I think she might still be here."

"You must mean Micky," she said. "There's not a lot of women here. Dante sells most of them to the highest bidder, but there are a few he keeps for himself."

Sick to her stomach at the possibilities this stranger spoke of, she had to know more. "Who's Dante?

"Dante is the boss around here," she answered as she looked over her shoulder to make sure she was alone. "I've never seen him though."

"You've never seen him? Would you know his voice if you heard it?" Maddie asked. Her questions doubled with each word this woman spoke. She had to move the conversation along to take advantage of her good luck.

"Yes, I would know him if I heard him. I would never forget that evil rasp that rose from his black heart."

"What is your name?" Maddie knew she found a light to brighten the dark night.

"It's Olivia."

"Olivia, I want you to listen to me carefully. I'm going to get you out of here, but I have to find Michelle." Maddie's heart broke as she listened to her story. The pain in Olivia's voice hovered just underneath her strong façade, a mask she wore every day. Any sign of weakness could get her and Tommy beaten, killed, or even worse in her mind, sold off.

"You won't find her here." She looked back at her through the gap, determined to give Maddie as much information as she could. "A man came and took her away about six months ago."

"A man? Do you know who the man was?"

"No, but he took her in the middle of the night. I heard his voice in her bedroom. When she screamed, I got up to help her, but he took her outside so fast. They went up that hill over there." Her finger emerged through the slat half an inch from Maddie's face. She pointed to high ground that was more of a mountain that a hill.

The longer they spoke, the more belabored and frightened Olivia's voice became. "We can't stay out any longer. Dante will know. I will suffer and you will die."

"Then let me in." Maddie pushed on the wooden fence to break a piece off big enough for her to wedge her slender body through, but it wouldn't budge.

Olivia looked around and waited a moment before she told Tommy to go inside with his sister.

"Follow me over here." She walked to her right about fifteen feet and stopped at a small opening out of direct line of sight. Shrubs and rocks made it look like just a bunch of meaningless brush with nothing to hide. She pulled away the debris and exposed an opening large enough to fit the well-fed cat that came to visit Tommy a few times a week, but even his fuzzy friend would struggle to fit through the tight space without leaving some fur behind.

"See if you can squeeze in here, but be careful. Are you a small person? I can't really see you."

"I'll get in," Maddie said, not convinced of her own assertion.

The space was taller than it was wide. She shimmied her way through inch by inch, the dirt mixed with some foreign substance that dug into her skin. The wood surrounding the narrow space was pliable from the rot that ate away at the edges of the plank, but the pieces were not breakable. Olivia was able to bend it just enough so Maddie could get through, but not without deep scratches that bled down her long legs.

"C'mon. Hurry. Stay down and crawl up the side of the porch behind the plants. I'll go up the front steps alone. When I open the door, you sneak inside."

Maddie was impressed with Olivia's resolve, keen instincts, and obvious mental toughness. An instant bond formed between them and common ground was not hard to find. She could tell there was something different about her.

The moment Maddie crawled inside the door she felt Michelle's essence. Even though she was no longer there, Maddie knew her sister had lived in this house.

"Are you okay?" Olivia asked, as she sat on the linoleum floor and cradled her as she did when Micky needed to feel safe. "You look just like her. Just like she said you did."

She was here. My sister was here. Maddie broke down.

"Why don't you come sit?" Olivia helped her to her feet. "Let me get you something to put on those terrible scratches."

The house was small and the interior was outdated by a century. The atmosphere was oddly comfortable, and the square-shaped room was filled with handmade crafts. Paper plates with smiley faces made of yarn covered a pink wall, and the smell of a homemade meal lingered in the air. Maddie stared at the smiles glued to the artwork wondering if the sentiment could be real, at least for the children.

"We don't have too much time before Dante's henchmen come around to check on us." She patted Maddie's wounds with gauze to soak up the blood, then applied a homemade ointment to help her heal.

"Okay, tell me what's going on here." Maddie pulled herself together and cut to the chase.

"Where to begin?" Olivia said. "I was a young girl working at my first real job selling financial products to wealthy individuals. I agreed to meet one of my best clients at his mansion late one night to sign some documents I needed executed by the morning. When I arrived, there were bags of drugs on his desk and three muscle-bound men beating him to a pulp."

"Olivia, I'm so sorry."

"It looked like he was dead. I will never know for sure. The three men scooped me up, put a sack over my head, and threw me into the back of a van. The next thing I knew, I was in this little house. I don't even know how long I've been here or even where we are." She looked around the space that had become her home. "It had to be at least six years ago because my son Tommy is five, but I think it's much longer than that. After a while, everything gets turned around on you and you can barely figure out what time it is. We aren't allowed to know that or anything else."

"So you had Tommy while you were held here?"

"Yes. Without him and Micky, I'd have gone crazy."

"You and Micky lived here in this house?"

"Yes. I love her. I always will," she said with her hand over her heart. "When she first came here, she was so scared and really shaken up. She could barely talk. We only had each other to lean on and we grew very close, like family. I taught her how to survive here and she taught me how to forgive."

"She was an angel on earth." Maddie concurred with Olivia's sentiment. "She didn't deserve what happened to her."

"Micky told me everything in bits and pieces over the years. Even after all the hurt she suffered, she still was able to forgive and the only person she was worried about in this world was you."

"Thank you for being there for her," Maddie said.

"She was there for me just as much." Olivia panted and grew more anxious as time ticked away. She had become an expert in judging time without a clock.

"Tell me about this place. Where can I find this… Dante?"

"I don't know much about the layout. We aren't allowed onto the dirt road that leads to the rest of the compound. There is no visual barrier, but an alarm goes off whenever someone crosses a certain point near the road and Dante's henchmen come running."

"Why haven't you escaped through the hole in the fence?" Maddie asked.

"He'd just find us and kill us. There is no escaping. No one can leave unless you have permission to leave."

"How do you get this permission?"

"You have to be sold. Someone has to buy you, but Micky and I were not for sale. I made sure she knew how to become one of the *special* ones. It's the only way to survive."

Maddie clenched her teeth to suppress the rage. "Okay," she continued with a short pause and an inspection of the living conditions. "It looks like you have plenty of food and supplies."

"Yes, Dante ordered his brother, Spider, bring us anything we need."

"That's very generous for hardened criminals like these people."

"Yes. I suppose it is. But..."

"But? What, Olivia?"

"Spider is Tommy's father," she said with her head bowed down in shame.

Maddie hugged her and assured her she need not feel shame for anything. "None of this is your fault. And besides..." she said in an effort to lift her spirits, "look at that beautiful little boy over there. He's happy and sweet as can be. That's all because of you."

"And Micky," Olivia said. "Micky is as much of a mother to Tommy as I am. Protecting him, teaching him, loving him."

"I'm not surprised." Olivia's words were proof that her sister's faith and good spirit remained strong in the midst of such horror. "I am going to take a look around the grounds and I'll get back in touch with you. I'll go to the same spot in the fence and slide a thin, leafy branch through the slat right over the opening. That's how you'll know I'm here, okay?"

"When will you be back?"

"Soon. I don't know how long it will take for me put a plan in play. We'll have only one shot to get you all out unharmed. We have to get it right."

"These are very dangerous people," she said, worried that no plan, no matter how well thought out, would ever free them from the animals' jaws.

"Very dangerous, yes, but once we get you and Tommy out I'll make sure you both are protected. You took Michelle under your wing. You taught her how to survive here, kept her safe for all these years from these barbarians. She could have been tortured, strung out on drugs, or worse. I owe you everything. Mark my words, they will pay." She took Olivia's hand and felt her tremble. "Check the fence regularly for my marker. Just keep an eye out, okay?"

"We will. For now, you'll have to go back out the way you came or you'll trip the alarm. As far as I know, that's the only time it goes off, when someone tries to enter the dirt road that leads to the house at the top of the hill. I don't know if you'll be able to get close enough to see anything."

"I'll find a way," Maddie said, confident she would be able to scope out the main house without being detected.

"Wait," Olivia stopped her before she dropped to the floor to crawl out. "There is someone else you should meet before you go."

Maddie looked at her in a state of confusion. *Is she turning me in?*

Olivia walked over to a handmade flower and paisley curtain that hung from the ceiling and covered a doorway to a hidden room inside the cube.

"Sweetheart, could you please come out here for a moment?" she said, with pure love for the treasure behind the curtain.

Out stumbled the most beautiful little girl Maddie ever saw. Her hair bounced up and down, pink and yellow bows held her pigtails in place.

Maddie loved her the moment she laid eyes on her, but didn't exactly know why. "Hi, sweetheart," she said, unable hold back her emotion. "You look so beautiful."

"Thank you," she answered, her small right foot stepped over her left to curtsy. "My mommy made me this dress."

Olivia turned to Maddie who sat near the door in silence and made the formal introduction. "Maddie, I'd like you to meet…Madison, Micky's daughter."

Madison ran into Maddie's arms almost on cue. She planted her little, four-year-old body onto hers and held on for dear life.

"You look just like my mommy," she said with a smile that would melt the world's largest glacier.

"I do?" Tears dripped onto her niece's simple, handmade pink dress.

"Yes. You're very pretty." She patted her on the head with her little hand.

"Why, thank you. But I'm not as pretty as you." Maddie and Madison rubbed noses. Maddie felt a kind of love she never felt before and knew her life had changed forever.

Using only her lips to form the words so the children would not hear, she asked, *Who is her father?*

Dante.

Maddie's heart stopped beating, if only for a minute.

"Okay, Madison, come on with me now. Maddie has to go now, but she'll be back."

"Wait, Auntie Olivia, I want to give her something. Can I go get it?"

"Yes, you can, sweetheart."

Madison skipped toward her room and disappeared behind the curtain. After less than a minute, she emerged with a small, leather bound book in her hand and handed it to Maddie. "This was my mommy's book. She read it to me every night."

It was Michelle's Bible, a special gift just for her given to her by their mother Gail, when she was about four years old. The message read, *God bless you and keep you safe. Love Mom and Dad.*

Madison gave Maddie another big hug and a kiss, and said, "Come back soon. We'll have a tea party." She skipped back toward the room and disappeared behind the curtain one more time; this time she did not return.

"She's so amazing. Thank you, Olivia, for taking care of her."

"Of course," she said. "I will protect her with my life. She is a bright, happy little girl."

"I promise you, I will get you, Tommy, and Madison out of here if it's the last thing I do here on earth."

"I know you will. As sure as I'm standing here, I know you will," she answered. "There is one thing you should keep in mind."

"What is it?"

"Micky knows things. Things no one else knows. Things she wouldn't even tell me for my own safety."

"How?"

"Dante and his goons are terrible people, but he adores his daughter. He'd kill for her. Micky and Madison were taken to the main house at the top of the hill a few times a week so Dante could spend time with his daughter. He never came down here."

"Did she ever tell you anything?"

"Every time she came back she'd just said that I would never believe what was going on up there and if she ever told anyone anything about what she saw or heard, Dante would make sure she never saw Madison again. He knew if he threatened to take Madison away, she would never talk."

With the final word, Olivia leaned down and kissed her on the forehead. Maddie gave her one last embrace and headed out to scope the grounds.

Maddie roamed the area for hours before she returned to the car with a plan to save her niece and her new family from living the rest of their lives as prisoners. Finding Michelle and exposing Dante was her only hope of saving them all.

CHAPTER FOURTEEN

Detective Hanoy's office at the police station provided the perfect location for Maddie to brief him and Jordan on the details of her plan. The trio headed back and worked into the wee hours of the morning. It was the only option, especially for Roger.

"As I see it, there is only going to be one way we can locate Michelle's whereabouts," Maddie said. "Colin has to lead us to her."

"You know that's going to be a tough order to fill," Roger answered.

"You have to get him to do it. Lie to him, you're good at that." Her patience was in short supply.

"So let's recap. Connor's letter said he arranged it so Colin would be able to see Michelle when he went to the compound. The letter also said that once he got there he'd be filled in on *the rest*. Then Olivia said she saw Michelle leave the compound with someone whom she'd never seen before. So the question is, what was *the rest* and who did she leave with? I think that Connor called in another favor and got Dante to release Michelle to Colin. But instead of bringing her back to Timberton, he locked her up somewhere, keeping her for himself."

"That's very possible," Roger said. "Colin has always been obsessed with her. And with his delusions growing worse as he gets older, his obsession is sure to become even more intense."

"And now Dante has my niece to hold over her head. I'm sure Michelle had no choice but to go along with whatever he wanted if she ever wanted to see her daughter again." She slapped her hand on the top of Roger's desk.

"It all makes perfect sense," Jordan said.

"Roger, in a few hours, say around nine a.m., we'll meet in front of Colin's hospital room, talk to him to find out what he knows." Maddie handed out the orders. "And if you don't show up, or cross me in any way, I will show you no mercy."

Jordan looked him straight in the eyes with an unmistakable warning to comply for his own sake.

With only a few hours until go time, Jordan and Maddie left Roger alone in his office to ruminate over the fact that his colleagues, wife, and children would soon know the truth and life as he knew it would cease to exist.

Back at the ranch, Ally fed her inner diva with a pool party made up of her ten closest bar friends. The empty bottles of alcohol reeked of a wild time and her inability to walk straight exposed her indulgence.

"Guys," she said as she stumbled toward the front door with a poor attempt to balance a tray of half-eaten pizza, stale potato chips, and a smattering of dried avocado dip. "You missed a great party. But good thing you weren't here, handsome man. You get a little too frisky with the ladies when you drink too much. My bestie doesn't like it when you drink too much."

"Okay, we've heard enough, crazy girl." Maddie took the tray out of her hand and spun her little bare body toward the stairs. "Let me help you to bed."

She took her upstairs and tucked her in under the puffy comforter Miss Camilla just cleaned earlier that day. The satin fabric released the scent of a dozen roses with every pat and every tuck.

"Rest up, girlfriend," she said. "I'll shut the shades. The sun is bright this morning."

Maddie had no plans to sleep, but a hot shower and some something cold to drink were on her radar. Fortunately for her, her sexy boyfriend had the same idea. A crystal carafe of ice water with oranges and lemons floating among the ice cubes invited her to take a sip and her alpha male's bare bottom tempted her into the bedroom.

"Come here." Jordan gave her an order for a change. "It's my turn."

"Is it really?" She defied his command and walked backward, playing hard to get.

"You're a bad girl," he said. Her playfulness aroused him and the thought of not being able to have her made him want her more.

"Maybe I am a bad girl. What are you gonna do about it, you big pussy cat?" She shed her clothes one piece at a time, leaving her scent for him to follow. Maddie shot him a come-hither glance as she headed for the rainbow shower, the beast ready to explore her lair. Ally would be sound asleep by now, so she was certain she wouldn't attack if they infiltrated her marked territory and used her mating cove.

Jordan walked by Ally's room with all his precious gear in tow. Ally had always seemed to know when a hot, naked male was within striking distance;

her radar remained engaged even in a state of sleep. She opened her eyes just enough to watch him pass by her open door. It wouldn't be the first time she'd caught him roaming the halls of his own house with all his glory hanging out, a fringe benefit she enjoyed during her stay.

Jordan and Maddie stood together in perfect harmony, a portrait of two people in love.

"I want to see every part of you." He spun her around with her arm extended high above her head like a graceful ballerina. "Look at you."

"Do you like me?" She was coy and irresistible.

"Do I like you? I love you. I'm in love with you. I want to make love to you right now." He took her hand in his, kissed her palm, and made a circle around his heart.

"Wait." She stopped him before she let herself go. "Is this really happening? Can you really ever be mine?"

"I am yours. I'll always be yours. I've always been yours," he said, as he leaned in and kissed her mouth with wet, full lips. There was no turning back. She believed him. She believed *in* him. She was ready to release her heart from the prison that had confined it for far too long.

"I love you too, Jordan," she said without breaking eye contact. "I mean it. I don't want anything to come between us. Promise me we start 'us' with no secrets and no lies."

He hesitated for just a moment, long enough for her to notice. The hesitation played tug of war in her mind, but her heart won the battle.

"Yes," he answered. "No secrets."

She dropped to her knees and took him in her mouth. He almost felt too guilty to continue, but her skill rendered him defenseless.

Every color of the rainbow flashed over her face from the lights that rotated above them while she took her time and showed him how much she loved to please him.

"You are incredible." He grabbed her head and went in deeper. "Don't stop." With only one more lick, he let himself go like never before.

He stood her up and held her flush against his body, not an inch of flesh separated.

The warm water trickled down on them from above. The stream that followed the path to her sweet spot did not hide her already wet paradise. She was eager for him to show her he loved her too.

She writhed with desire. Her back landed flat against the tile wall with her hips pressed forward to meet his flesh, but he pulled away just enough to tease her and make her want him even more. She never felt sexier, more turned on, or more loved than she did at this moment. He built her up like nothing she had even known, and he was not about to disappoint her.

"You feel so good inside," he said as he entered her one gentle thrust at time.

His large, masculine hands moved her hips in a slow circular motion on the tip of his shaft. Her arms stretched out around him, bracing herself for the pleasure she'd longed to achieve.

"Give me all of you. Please!" Water dripped between her cheeks.

Her muscles contracted and he emptied himself inside her.

She hung onto him, unable to stand. He held her in his arms until she regained her strength.

"I want you to stay. Build your life here, again. With me."

"I want that to. I do."

Jordan and Maddie spent the next few minutes in each other's arms and listened to her favorite song.

He would do anything to have her back, even if it meant he would have to live the rest of his life with the guilt of his dirty little secret.

Just two hours until she came face to face with Colin again, Maddie's blood ran rapid with adrenaline, determined not to let anything stand in the way of a new life with Jordan, Michelle, and her niece, Madison.

"Hello, is Mr. Jordan there?" Miss Camilla knocked on the bedroom door.

"Yes, Miss Camilla. I'm here. Is everything okay?"

She waved Jordan into the hallway so Maddie wouldn't hear the announcement she'd been asked to make. "Mr. Jordan, Miss Eliza is downstairs and is demanding to see you right away. She threated to run up here and find you herself if I didn't do what she asked."

"It's okay, you did the right thing. Please tell her I will be right down." He gave Miss Camilla an approving pat on the shoulder.

While Maddie dried her hair and dressed in the bathroom, Jordan walked downstairs three steps at a time ready to get rid of Eliza for the last time.

"I need you to leave," he said without a care as to why she wanted to see him.

"Jordan, I want to talk. You owe it to me to at least hear what I have to say."

"No, actually I don't owe you anything. After the stunt you pulled, you're lucky I don't have security throw you out on your ass."

"You're right. I should not have stolen the velvet bag from her room. That was wrong, but you've changed since she returned. I saw the way you looked at her in the stables that day and it made me crazy, I acted crazy." Eliza hoped he would remember the good times they shared.

"You are dead to me. You crossed the line. I want you to leave." There is nothing you can say or do that will make me want you back."

"You're with *her* now, aren't you?" She slammed her purse on the sofa with such force the contents spilled out onto the floor. "Don't even deny it."

"Yes. Just leave it alone."

"Did you tell your fuck buddy about your affair with her beloved sister? I'll bet she'd like to know you were screwing her behind her back, wouldn't she?"

"You better not even think about going toe to toe with me," he said. "You will lose and your father will go down with you. If you don't want him to suddenly find his corrupt business dealings all over the news, you'll walk away."

"What corrupt dealings? My father is one of the most honest men I know and his company is one of the most successful venture capital companies around."

"You are so naïve, Eliza." He laughed finding it hard to take her seriously. "You go ahead and keep believing that. But I can assure you, your father is as crooked as they come."

"Then what does that make you and your father?"

Jordan did not dignify her accusation with a response and regretted the day he ever let his father talk him into asking this venomous snake to marry him.

"Listen to me right now. You are going to turn around, leave us alone, and keep your mouth shut. Do you understand me?'

"Jordan?" She pleaded one last time, unsure who this man was who stood in front of her. Some of their fights could rival the ugliest battles of all times, but she never saw him turn to steel. Maddie was the catalyst.

"Not one more word. Go."

"You are going to regret this day," she said as she picked up her belongings from the living room floor.

"Leave." He shut the door behind her with such force, the sound echoed through the quiet early morning air.

"Who was at the door?" Maddie asked with a noticeable spring in her step as she bounced down the winding staircase looking more stunning than usual. Her studded blue jeans, brown leather cowboy boots, and her signature white tank top were understated, but spoke volumes.

"Eh, just a delivery. No big deal. I took care of it."

Maddie was drawn to the kitchen by the smell of the freshly brewed coffee Miss Camilla had prepared. "I could drink the whole pot." She indulged herself in a hefty dose of the caffeine delicacy.

"Come on over here you sexy thing. Sit on big daddy's lap."

"I'm coming. Just a minute. I have a feeling this is going to be quite a day. I need a little more sugar in my coffee this morning."

She walked over with her extra sweet morning pick-me-up and took a sip while she lowered herself onto his masculine thighs. She was careful not to pounce in case the force of her landing would aggravate his leg that had not yet fully returned to its original condition.

He wrapped his protective arms around her. His gentle caress up and down her back sent tingles down her spine. "Are you ready for this?" he asked.

"I've never been more ready," she said. "Let's do this."

It was as if the checkered flag signaled a racecar driver to step on the gas. She jumped up, ordered Jordan to grab his things and meet her outside by the car. He was not about to suggest anything different.

Jordan and Maddie made it to the hospital with time to spare. Hoping that Roger might also be ahead of schedule, they stood in front of Colin's room with the security guards well before the nine o'clock hour.

"Where the hell is he?" Maddie asked Jordan as she paced the hall. "If Roger screws us, he'll be sorry he ever met me."

"He'll be here. He's a lot of things, but stupid isn't one of them."

Nine o'clock came and went, and Maddie was fit to be tied. Ring after ring, she blew up his phone with one call after another, no pause between each attempt.

At half past nine, Jordan saw Roger limping down the corridor. "Here he comes."

Maddie turned toward Roger, ready to unleash her inner ninja on him. Jordan was forced to restrain her with his body. He held her from behind to keep her from an assault charge, or worse.

"Calm down. You have to calm down right now. We need him," he said into her ear. "Stop it."

"Where the hell have you been?" She poked Roger in the chest, the kindest welcome she could muster.

"I'm sorry I'm late. Please, calm down."

"Detective Hanoy, is there a problem here?" the door guards asked, ready to step in and detain her.

Roger hesitated for a moment and said, "No problem. We're fine." He signaled the guards to back down with a few waves of his hand.

"I was talking with my sister. Colin's mother. I thought she might be able to help. Maybe she could tell me something I don't know, something I could use. But she was half in the bag, another issue altogether."

"Why didn't you just call to tell us? Damn it. I didn't think you were going to show," Maddie said under her breath so only he could hear.

"Listen, I'm going to make this right if I can. I told you that. You're just going to have to trust me."

"Trust you? You're kidding, right?" Her desire to strangle him was apparent, but she had no choice but to find a way to let him have some rope. If he hung himself, she would be the first person to make sure it was not a failed attempt.

"Now you both wait out here for a minute. I'm going in to talk to him first."

"No way. I'm going in there with you."

"Maddie, let him go in first. He's right. If we want to get the story, we're going to have to let him go in alone," Jordan said.

She stared at Roger in silence for a hot minute. *Can I trust him?* The answer was no. *Is this too much rope? Maybe.*

If she had not put so much blind trust in Roger when she first returned to Timberton and sat with him in the diner, she might have seen through him from the start.

"Damn it. Just for the record, I don't like it, but I do think you should go in by yourself first. He'll talk to you without getting worked up. But I want you to record every word, and I mean every word. No breaks in the recording, no dead air, no excuses or you are finished. Do you understand?"

"Fair enough," he said.

"Good. I'm glad we understand each other."

Roger prepared his cell phone to record the conversation, walked in the room, and shut the door behind him.

Colin lay still, his head cocked toward the window as he stared off into space. He didn't even flinch at the squeaky door that announced a visitor.

"Colin?" Roger approached him with a pause in between each step so he would not startle him.

He turned his head toward his uncle, his eyes sullen, weary, and hollow. Roger couldn't help but feel for his nephew. Colin pulled at the handcuffs that dug into his skin and cut his wrists with every ferocious tug. He was desperate to free himself of the physical constraints that held his body hostage and the cage in his mind that held him prisoner.

"Colin." His uncle set the cell phone on the side table close enough to record every word. "How are you feeling?"

His question was met by a blank stare.

"The doctors say you are doing better. The medicine seems to be working."

Colin turned his head away and resumed his gaze into nothingness. Roger walked around the other side of the bed to force Colin to look at him.

"Colin. Do you remember what happened? Do you know why you're here?"

Colin's quick movement startled Roger. His head snapped, his face positioned parallel to the ceiling.

"Colin, are you okay?" He touched his arm. "What's wrong?"

"Michelle is out. Michelle is out." Colin chanted with an eerie rhythm.

"What do you mean, 'Michelle is out'?"

"She's out. I'll save her. I'll save her." The chant grew softer and less rhythmic.

"I don't know what you mean. What are you saying?" Roger asked in an effort to keep him engaged before his mind wandered away again.

"They will kill her. Kill her!" His arms and legs thrashed up and down; his handcuffs dug deeper into his wrists, blood poured from the gashes.

Roger stuck his head out the door and ordered Maddie to get a doctor in here right away. She wanted to bust into the room, but went for the doctor instead.

"Colin, I've called someone to come and settle you down," Roger said, as he patted him on the head to comfort him. "Can you calm down for me?"

A medical team ran into the room. The doctor instructed the nurses to hold the patient still so he could administer a sedative and get him under control. It didn't take long before the thrashing dissipated and his breathing slowed.

"I think you'll have to leave, sir."

"Doctor, if I may, I need just a few more minutes. This prisoner has vital information and time is of the essence. A girl's life is at stake."

The doctor took Colin's vital signs, checked his chart, and cleared the detective to continue his questioning. "Under the circumstances I will allow a few more minutes, but no more than that. Understood?"

"Yes, sir. I will be brief."

The team exited the room.

With little time left, Roger started right in. "Colin, can you tell me what happened when you went to see Michelle on the compound?"

His answer was coherent and calm, and his sentence structure was more fitting for a scholar rather than a prisoner under arrest for attempted murder. All of a sudden, it seemed as if a different person lay in this bed.

"I removed her from the compound with Dante's permission. He gave her to me as a favor to Connor."

Afraid he'd lose his cooperation, Roger got right to the point. "Where did you take her?"

"She's safe as long as she's with me. Dante made me promise I'd watch her. Make sure she didn't talk. He'll kill her if she talks. I'm going to protect her and make sure that doesn't happen," he said as if his story was typical of the average person's daily life.

"Where is she?"

"I can't tell you. No one can know," he said.

In an effort to appeal to his love for her, his uncle pointed out that given his condition, someone would have to bring her food, water, and watch over her. If he could just convince Colin to let him do it, he'd have to disclose her location.

"Let me help you," Roger said. "You love her. You want to see her again, don't you?"

"Yes, I love her."

"Then let me help you. You promised Dante you'd watch her. Who's watching her now? Do you even know where she is? You said she got out."

"No!" Colin appeared confused by Roger's logic. "Okay, calm down."

Out of nowhere, Colin presented Roger an offer he couldn't refuse. "I will take you there. We won't tell anybody. You can bring me there, Uncle Roger. We'll bring her food and sit and watch her, okay?"

Roger felt like he'd hit the jackpot and was run over by a truck at the same time. He remained coolheaded and answered as if his offer could remain a secret. "Sure. Yeah. We can do that. Just give me a minute and I'll call us a ride. How far is it from here would you say?"

"I don't know. Hours."

"Okay, sure. I'll be right back."

Roger stepped outside the door and asked Jordan and Maddie to follow him. The trio took the elevator to the second floor where there was an empty conference room.

"Apparently she's alive and he's going to take me to her. Listen to this," he said as he played the recording.

Maddie and Jordan could not believe what they heard, but were concerned Colin was still a loose cannon. The trigger that caused him to want to kill anyone who he saw as a threat to Michelle could reappear at any time.

"Great work, Roger. How quickly can we get on the road?"

"I'm going to get Colin released into my custody. I'll inform the staff that Judge Rollins ordered Colin to have a full psych evaluation at Bunker County Hospital in the next town. I'll drive with him in my cruiser. You and Jordan follow close behind."

"Is any of that true? About the judge? The evaluation?" Jordan asked.

"No." Roger walked out of the room to get the ball rolling.

"I've never been so happy to hear Roger lie," Maddie said with a sarcastic laugh.

Roger put the next phase of the plan into motion and broke every rule in the book to do it. *Ah, what*

difference does a few more felony charges make at this point?
I'm screwed no matter how you look at it.

Within the hour, Colin was in Roger's vehicle.
Jordan and Maddie followed them, but were careful
not to drive too close to Roger's car in case Colin was
keen enough to notice.

"Where are we going, Colin?" Not knowing what
was in store or who they might be dealing with,
Roger hoped to get more information before they
arrived on the scene.

"Just drive." Colin's disorientation and aggressive nature was returning. The detective could only
hope, for everyone's sake, he was not leading him on
a wild goose chase.

An hour into the drive, Colin's behavior grew more
peculiar. "Why is this taking so long?" He rocked
back and forth in passenger seat. "We have to get
there. I have to see if she's there. She got out. She
got out."

"It's okay, I'll drive faster. Here, see?" Roger said.
"Much faster."

"That's better." The faster Roger drove, the slow-
er he rocked.

Jordan sped up to keep pace with them. The roads became narrow and civilization disappeared.

"Where does that bastard have her?" Maddie said. She saw nothing but dirt, trees, and Roger's vehicle not far ahead.

⇥ ⇤

"Stop here," Colin said with no warning.

Roger slammed on the brakes and stopped on a dime.

Luckily for Jordan, he'd left enough distance between them to compensate for the quick stop without Colin noticing their tail.

"Here. We get out here."

"Here?" Roger looked around at the forest.

"Yes, we have to walk from here." Colin pointed north and walked around to the trunk to get the knapsack of food and supplies Roger prepared at his request.

The terrain would be a formidable challenge with Roger's limp, but he was determined to go all the way no matter how far or how long it took. A quick glance over his shoulder gave him visual confirmation that Jordan and Maddie were ready to follow on foot.

"Hurry, let's go," Colin said as he jumped over the first few logs in their path.

The hike was exhausting. Sticks scratched their legs. Bugs, snakes, and unrecognizable critters met them at every turn. This was no walk in the park. Colin didn't rest for a second. And Roger kept up pretty well for an old chap who had a deep-seated fear of getting lost in the woods.

The forest was thick with brush. Roger was completely turned around. He knew he'd never find his way back without help. He only hoped Jordan and Maddie wouldn't leave him tied to a tree somewhere if this all went wrong.

Soon the brush thinned out and an excavated area about the size of a football field appeared. The evergreens were cleared from the wide-open space and large rocks were piled along the perimeter. Graded trenches were apparent. More than one backhoe, bulldozer, dump truck, and a plethora of building supplies worthy of a large-scale project waited to be used.

"What the hell is going on here?" Jordan said, curious about the extravagant operation out here in the middle of nowhere.

"I don't know, but we're going to find out," Maddie said.

Colin walked to the far corner of the cleared-out space. There stood a large trailer affixed to the ground. The boarded-up windows and industrial-size locks kept its contents safe from unwanted visitors.

"Look, Jordan." She pointed to the trailer. "Michelle must be in there."

"Stay cool and quiet." Jordan grabbed her hips to stop her from crawling too far into the line of sight. "Let Roger get inside first. Then we'll go in and get her out of there."

"Yeah, you're right." She focused on Colin who stood near the entrance.

"Stay here. I'm going back to the car to get my gun," Jordan said.

"I didn't know you brought a gun."

"Just stay still. Promise me."

"Okay," She crossed her fingers like a little kid. "I will."

Colin went into the woods and came out with a rack of at least fifty keys. He selected one to open the door. The padlock disengaged with one turn of the key.

He opened the door, stepped inside, and lit a candle. There was no electricity, but the weather was warm enough to keep Michelle from freezing even though the nights were cold and uncomfortable.

Colin instructed Roger to wait outside the trailer door. Roger looked around and didn't see Jordan or Maddie, but felt their stare and their urge to raid the structure.

After about five minutes, Colin invited Roger in. He took one last scan of the open space to see if he could catch a glimpse of his *friends* in the distance and then shut the door behind him.

The deplorable, repulsive conditions inside the trailer caused Roger's gut to churn. The stench of dead carcasses, garbage, and urine nearly made him pass out. The filth was unlike anything he'd ever seen. Colin, however, seemed unaffected by the repugnant, rotting odor of food and the grisly conditions he forced Michelle to endure.

"Michelle?" Roger walked over to a figure hunched up in the corner, stepping over dead rodents and crushing roaches with his shoes. "Honey, come here. I'm going to help you. Come. Please."

Michelle didn't say a word, but got up from a small area in the corner she'd cleared out so she could sit without the squalor under her feet.

"Let's go, dear," Roger said. He guided her away from decaying flesh from the animals Colin expected her to cook with a battery-operated hot plate. "Don't look down. Look straight ahead."

"Where do you think you're going?" Colin blocked their path to the only exit.

"We are going outside for a minute," Roger said, unable to look Colin in the eye after seeing the torture he had inflicted on this poor, innocent girl.

"No! You aren't going anywhere. Go back!"

"We are going outside." Roger said. He remained calm in an attempt to deescalate his aggression while he continued to lead Michelle toward the door, his arm wrapped around her shoulder and her chafed, scabbed hand placed in his.

"No! I said go back!" Colin pushed Michelle onto an old, torn chair and knocked over the candle, causing the piles of debris to ignite.

Roger wrestled with Colin to give Michelle a chance to run out the door, but she was frozen with fear. He grabbed Colin by the throat and pinned him against the fake wood paneling. Colin punched the old man in the stomach and tackled him like he was a three-hundred-pound linebacker in a playoff game. The two opponents fell out the door onto the grass, both men wrapped up like a pretzel. By the time Maddie saw the two tumble out of the doorway, she was already half way to the trailer. Jordan had not yet returned from the car with the loaded gun, but the smoke that emanated from the trailer was reason enough to break her promise to stay still until he returned.

"Roger!" Maddie's legs carried her at a record speed.

He flipped Colin over on top of him and applied a combat grade chokehold. With his back to the dirt, he let out a loud cry. "Go in and get her out!"

"Michelle!" Maddie waded through the thick, black smoke. "Where are you? It's your sister! I'm here!"

The fire tore through the hellhole and engulfed it with suffocating flames. There was little air to breathe.

Colin landed a powerful elbow to Roger's gut that broke him free from his old uncle's hold. He ran up the stairs and padlocked the only way in or out, both girls locked inside. There was no way for Madison or Michelle to escape the explosion of flames.

Roger reached for the key rack lying on the dirt, but with no less than fifty keys on it, he could not find the right one.

"You will never take her from me!" In a psychotic state of rage, Colin charged at his uncle again, this time with a sharp metal spike that lay on the ground. He missed his chest by inches.

Roger drew his 9mm pistol from his side holster and shot Colin between the eyes, killing him instantly.

Roger let out a yell that could be heard across the nation. "Jordan! Help!"

Flames flared, black smoke so thick he could not see a foot in front of him. He banged on the singed sills and used his bad leg to balance himself while he kicked in a low, small, boarded-up window with his good leg. Only a small piece of screen fell off. The girls banged the window from the other side. Roger knew right where they were.

"Jordan!" Roger could not believe what he saw rolling across the empty ditch.

Out of a bunker in the woods came Jordan driving one of the front-end loaders toward the inferno. Roger signaled Jordan to drive it to the far end of the trailer to avoid the area where the girls remained trapped. In one fell swoop, Jordan obliterated the structure as if it was made of grains of sand and created an opening for the girls to escape.

"Thank you, God," Roger said as he looked up to heaven and dropped to his knees.

Madison and Michelle emerged from the fiery hellhole. Each breath of air was a gift. With hair singed and burns that covered sixty percent of their body, the sisters held on to each other with no intention to ever let go no matter how much it hurt their melted flesh.

Jordan ran to the girls to help them, emergency personnel already dispatched. He sat with them until first responders arrived. "Help is on the way. We're gonna be all right."

CHAPTER FIFTEEN

Two tumultuous weeks passed since the medevac helicopter touched down on the remote dirt patch that hid Colin's filthy house of horrors. During the same agonizing weeks, Maddie and Michelle spent a countless number of hours in the hospital for their second- and third-degree burns. Doctors confirmed the burns would heal with the proper care, but the recovery from the years of emotional and psychological trauma would take a lifetime.

Michelle had the longest road back to a normal life. Her fragile condition was controlled with medication and sedation. Only one thought consumed her. Her daughter. The idea of innocent, young

Madison's fate in the hands of one of the most notorious criminals of their time was too much for Michelle to bear. With her daughter's life still at risk, a hole bored through her heart, a void that no one could fill and no medication could numb. She prayed every second of every day that she would hold her again and she'd be safe from the evil that lived within the compound walls.

Maddie didn't let Michelle out of her sight, their hospital beds pushed together, and rolled apart only when the nurses changed their bandages or administered medication. Her sister was frail and had sustained injuries that were much more severe. Maddie didn't want to push her, but she knew they had to act soon. Despite Jordan's influence with the media to keep Michelle's rescue concealed, it would only be a matter of time before it got out.

Maddie told Michelle everything she'd discovered while they lay in their hospital beds. She recounted how she infiltrated the compound by her fortunate encounter with Tommy, the kindness she received from Olivia, and the most important moment of all, meeting her sweet, little niece Madison.

Michelle couldn't speak yet due to the severe injuries she'd suffered in the fire and was forced to communicate using a small chalkboard.

When Maddie mentioned Madison, her face lit up the room with the only smile that had adorned her blistered face since the rescue. She pulled out her tablet and filled it with questions. *You saw her? Is she okay? Is Olivia still watching her? Is she safe? Is she eating? Is she happy?*

Her hand continued to fill the blackboard with questions until it stopped in midair, the worn down, yellow piece of chalk fell to the floor and her head dropped. She felt a wave of pain only a mother could know.

The last words to appear on her tablet read *I want my daughter back. You have to find her, Please!*

"I will get her back. I promise you as sure as I am here in front of you."

Michelle wrote down everything about her traumatic life. Her intricate account covered every inch of the board. The facts she disclosed could bring down the entire crime ring and put a target on her family's back. The information was for her sister's eyes only and she erased each sentence as Maddie read it. Dante's men infiltrated every corner of society and she begged her sister to trust no one.

Dante and his men will find me, she wrote; tears stung each wound as they trickled down her face. *I know too much. As long as I stayed with Colin, Dante would honor his deal with Connor. His loyalty to his men is fierce. But now, he will come after me, us, my daughter.*

"We have the best security money can buy," Maddie said.

The chalk scratched the board as if she was writing with her nails. *It won't matter. He will use my daughter. He will win!*

"No," she answered. "He won't win. We will get Madison, Olivia, and Tommy back and bring down the bastard. He won't be able to hurt you anymore. I promise you."

Jordan and Roger put a complex plan into action to ensure everyone's safety while Maddie recovered. Roger recruited an impressive team of highly trained officers to guard the girls and the Pike family until Dante's organization was brought to justice.

Even though Roger had come through on his promises so far, Jordan was not willing to put all his trust in him.

To ensure all the bases were covered, Jordan hired a fleet of former United States Navy SEALs headed by Commander McFarley and armed them with military grade fully automatic assault rifles and other firearms to protect the ranch. Jordan's connections never came in so handy. For even more protection, he assembled an additional team of men with the same skills and resources as a backup and stationed them right outside Maddie and Michelle's hospital room door. Jordan needed special permission from the hospital muckety-mucks to pull off such a feat, but since Kingston Enterprises donated all of the funds to build the hospital's Surgical Center, he had no problem getting their full cooperation.

As soon as the doctor cleared the girls to receive visitors, Gail, Larry, Brandon, and Ally rushed to the hospital to see them. Michelle was in much worse condition than Maddie. Their knees buckled when they saw Michelle for the first time. Larry caught Gail in midair to keep her from landing on the floor. Michelle's scars ravaged her conscience.

"My sweet, special baby girl. You are home now." Gail outlined Michelle's bandaged face with her hands. Her mother kissed her on the forehead and suffocated from her own tears. Larry, Brandon, and Ally searched for inner strength, but there was none.

The emotion was palpable. Sorrow turned to relief, relief turned to fear, fear turned to anger, anger led to questions, and the cycle continued for more than an hour. When the clock hit eight and the sun faded, the doctors entered their room to examine the patients and prescribe some much-needed rest.

Michelle's pain medication caused her to fall sleep almost instantly, but Maddie could not sleep.

"If it were not for Jordan's quick thinking and his ability to hotwire anything and everything, we would have never escaped that death trap." She spoke to herself, but not loud enough to wake Michelle. Maddie knew she owed him her life, their lives. She wanted to live hers—with him.

Morning followed faster than anyone preferred.

"Good morning, ladies," Dr. Ollie Benton said, a world-renowned burn specialist Jordan hired to check on them. "I know this has been quite an ordeal. However, you are both progressing quite well. We will be releasing you in a few days. Mr. Kingston arranged for your follow-up care and you will be well taken care of, I can assure you." Confident strokes of his pen followed his verbal assessment. He asked them several more questions, then left them to rest until lunchtime.

⇒⁓ ⁓⇐

The media got wind of the twins' approximate release date. Media crews crowded the parking lot. Chaos wreaked havoc through the area and reporters descended like hawks hunting for prey. This was the biggest story Timberton had ever seen. Everyone wanted a piece of it. Even the curiosity of the good people of Timberton contributed to the unwanted attention, but the Pikes were loved by all and well-wishers came out in droves to show their support.

Ally struggled to get past the crowd of reporters, microphones shoved in her face left and right on her way into the facility. The media storm escalated daily, but this morning was the worst day yet.

"Hi, my sisters whom I love so much." Ally bounced in with her customary bag of goodies and fancy toiletries, giving the girls big but careful hugs so she would not disturb the bandages.

"Hi, Ally." Michelle struggled to get the words out. She managed to force a slow mumble clear enough to understand.

"I'm impressed," Ally said. The swelling and blisters that crippled her speech were healing faster than expected.

"How are you ladies?" She opened a bottle of Maddie's favorite sparkling water and placed two bottles on the hospital tray for each of them without asking if they wanted it. "I gave a bottle to the hunky guards on the way in. They love me."

"We're doing okay." Maddie answered so Michelle wouldn't move her mouth too much, too fast. "I haven't had a chance to thank you for everything you've done for me. You are a true friend and I am so grateful to have you in my life."

"You know I'd do anything for you."

"But you've given up a lot to be here with me. You put up with calls from Richard, put your business on hold, referred away your new clients, I mean, I could go on. It's really incredible and selfless of you. I just want you to know how much I appreciate what you've done. It's a big deal."

"Thank you, and I'd do it all again," she said. "I love you, girl."

"I love you too."

The media frenzy that grew outside only confirmed Maddie's decision to recover at the ranch rather than turn her parents' home into a fortress, even though Larry and Gail assured her they could handle it. She couldn't have her ill mother exposed to this kind of stress. It would only get more chaotic and more dangerous from here on in.

Maddie felt the safest place for them was to stay with Jordan and divert attention away from her parents, not that Jordan would have allowed her to consider any other option. The ranch's state of the art security system, locked gates, massive police presence, and Jordan's security team would provide the safety, seclusion, and privacy everyone needed.

The girls' release was scheduled to take place sometime in the next few days. Roger arranged for an unmarked police escort to accompany the twins to the ranch, complete with roadblocks that extended for miles to keep the media away from the entrance. Jordan would remain at the ranch to receive them so he would not draw any additional unwanted attention to the transfer.

Maddie hadn't determined Roger's fate yet. For now, she'd kept his criminal acts a secret from the world as she promised in exchange for his help.

"Miss Camilla? Are you in there?" Jordan walked from his living room through the kitchen to the laundry room, looking for her to make a very important request.

"Yes, Mr. Jordan. I'm here," she answered while she folded laundry that emanated that clean, fresh scent.

"Did I ever tell you how much I appreciate you?" he asked, followed by a big hug.

"Oh yes. I'm very happy here. How is Miss Maddie and Miss Michelle today?"

"They will be released this week and will come here to live with us," he said.

"I'm so happy for that. I want to tell them they are in my prayers," she said with her hands pressed together. She adored Maddie and was anxious to welcome Michelle into the house.

"Miss Camilla, I'm going to give them my room to share. So, Brandon and some of my buddies are coming over to move things out of my room and move in the new bedroom suite of furniture I bought for them."

"Oh that is a good idea, Mr. Jordan. Miss Maddie will appreciate that."

"It will be good for them to stay together for a while. It's the largest bedroom on the ranch and has the best view of the horses. My girls should feel comfortable."

"Yes, they will love it. I'll prepare all the fixings for them. Don't you worry." She gave him a wink. "I know she likes my bath oils and the smell of the soap I use on her sheets."

"That she does. Thank you." He winked back.

Jordan's surprise accommodations should go off without a hitch with help from his friends. And Ally's design expertise will transform his bedroom from a man's playground to a whimsical, Victorian sanctuary.

He knew how important it was to Maddie to stay with Michelle at all times. *I think she's going to be really happy.* He jumped over the staircase rail as if he was leaping a fence.

⋯

The day everyone had been waiting for finally arrived.

"I'm going to head over to help the girls prepare to leave this morning," Ally said to Jordan as she ran through the kitchen with purse in hand. She scooped up a cup of aromatic coffee and stuffed a hot, glazed cinnamon bun in her mouth.

"Come sit here for a second," he said. He waved her over to the dining room table where he had finished his breakfast of eggs sunny-side up and grilled bacon drenched in maple syrup. The scent of the country bacon and warm syrup mixed together drew her in, but not as much as Jordan's sexy morning appearance. His cowboy hat, pressed red and black plaid shirt, and low-rise jeans gave proper credit to his well-earned physique.

"Is there something wrong with me? I haven't hit on you in at least three days," she laughed, a piece of bacon hanging from the side of her mouth.

"No, there's nothing wrong with you." He laughed at her self-assessment. "You've done everything right."

Flattered by his compliment, Ally felt her cheeks turn a bright red.

"You're a special friend to Maddie and have become a great friend of mine. I have prepared a big surprise for her and I want you to be part of it."

"Really? I'm honored. What is it?"

"I am going to ask her to marry me. You are the first person to know."

"Wow, Jordan. That is freaking fantastic news." She was happy for him and even happier for her best friend.

"I want to keep it between you, me, and Maddie until this whole ordeal is behind us. I want her to be able to share this with you because I know she won't want to let herself be happy about it until Michelle and Madison are secure and safe. I know her. I could wait to ask, but I want her to know she has me in her corner forever. No matter what."

"She'll be so happy, Jordan. It will give her the strength to deal with all that's to come. I think it's great news and good timing."

"I'm also going to tell her I'd like Michelle and Madison to live here with us."

"This just keeps getting better. You are amazing. She is so lucky to have a man like you."

"I have one more request of you?"

"Please, ask away." She grabbed another piece of maple-covered bacon right off his plate.

"I want you to move into the ranch too. Permanently."

"Jordan, what?"

"Move in. She would want that. And I want that."

"I don't know what to say!"

"Say yes."

Ally had to pinch herself to make sure she was awake. She felt like this was the best offer she'd ever received from anyone in her life. It was as if he knew she wanted a change from her hectic life in New York even though they'd never discussed it.

"Yes!" She leaped up and gave him the biggest bear hug she could. "Thank you. I'm beside myself. I feel so fortunate."

"You're welcome. We are the fortunate ones. We'll work out the details later. Now go get our girls and bring them home." He tipped his black cowboy hat to her.

"On my way." She grabbed one more piece of syrup-saturated bacon from his plate and out the door she went.

The police caravan escorted Jordan's special ladies home without incident. Maddie was impressed with the fortress Jordan created. Just when she didn't think she could love him any more than she already did, he captured a piece of her she didn't know existed until now.

"How are my girls?" Jordan welcomed them inside with a gentle hand and a kiss on the cheek. The sight of Michelle's body, still wrapped in tight gauze to protect the deep wounds, softened his tough exterior and a wave of sadness came over him. Her more serious wounds were not visible while she lay in her hospital bed. The extent of her injuries was not evident to him until now.

"We are glad to be home." Maddie melted into his arms. Her small frame almost disappeared in his embrace.

"I love you. You are my life, my world, my purpose," he said.

The fleet of live-in registered nurses, certified aides, and physical therapists Jordan commissioned to care for the girls during their recovery lined up at the entrance in full uniform ready to execute the care plan. Michelle would need much more attention, both physically and psychologically, than Maddie, but the staff was prepared to attend to all their needs.

"Okay everyone, let's get them comfortable. Everyone knows their role here today, so let's please get started," Jordan said. "Maddie, if I could escort you upstairs for a minute?"

"Michelle, I'll be right back. Will you be all right?" She left her in the capable and trustworthy hands of Ally and the exceptional nurses.

Jordan carried Maddie up the circular staircase as if she were a new bride. A sentiment he would soon fulfill.

"This is nice." She hung on to him and rested her head on his firm, warm chest. She never wanted to let go.

Jordan pushed open his bedroom door with his cowboy boot, exposing the inner sanctum.

"Jordan!" She gasped at the sight of the elegant space. "This is incredible."

"It's for you. All for you." He kissed her as if it was their first time.

"It's so beautiful." The moment he placed her feet on the floor she executed a perfect pirouette. "I feel like a princess."

The twentieth century-themed room was one of Ally's most impressive creations to date. Dark, rich, and romantic colors complemented the mahogany wood accented with floral carvings, and velvet rose-colored curtains cascaded from the ceiling, long golden fringe flowing down to a puddle of fabric that circled the floor. Judge and Jury cuddled up beneath the sill making themselves right at home. The fluffy pair gave the room an extra warmth, perfect for the big reveal.

Jordan laid Maddie down with great care on top of the Victorian-style embroidered comforter he had specially designed with her favorite colors, her small frame immersed in the plush pile. The king-size bed with traditional posts and a draped canopy adorned with tassels made her feel romantic, a sharp contrast from her modern New York apartment that fed her wilder side.

"Do you like it?" Jordan asked while he drew a line around her face and over her tender lips with his forefinger.

"It's more than amazing," she said, his pinkie the recipient of a gentle bite.

"This makes me very happy, Maddie."

"Where will Michelle be sleeping?" She looked around the room for another bed.

"Right here." Jordan drew back a floor-to-ceiling curtain to expose another design masterpiece. "This is Michelle's bed."

"Oh, Jordan!" Tears welled up in her content eyes. "You outdid yourself. She is going to love this."

"She's been through hell all these years. We all have. Now we are home. Once we bring her daughter home, our family will be complete."

"I love the way you're talking." Maddie kissed him with every fiber of her being.

"A little later, maybe in a few days after you have a chance to rest, I have something I want to ask you."

"What is it?" She sat herself up.

"Not now." He laid her back down. "Just relax. I'll have them bring Michelle upstairs so you can get acquainted with your new surroundings."

"Okay. I can't wait for her to see this. Will you bring her up?"

"Yes, if that's what you want." He kissed her one last time.

"Oh, and Jordan?"

"Yes, my princess?"

"I have something to tell you too, later."

He nodded, closed the door behind him, and headed downstairs to get Michelle himself.

The girls rested in their room for the remainder of the day. Michelle was overwhelmed with gratitude, but her fear for her daughter's safety casted a dark shadow over her own rescue and thoughts of any future. For her, there was no future without Madison.

In the two weeks that followed the girls' release from the hospital, Jordan returned to work at Kingston Enterprises, and Maddie and Michelle spent as much time as they could with Larry, Gail, and Brandon to make up for lost time. The topic of Gail's failing health would have to wait for a later date. Michelle's fragile state of mind would not sustain another blow. Gail could only hope she would live long enough to meet her granddaughter and see her family together one last time.

The special task force worked tirelessly to gather intel to use against Dante. The operation's top priority was to extract Michelle's daughter and her friends first before a takedown of the entire organization.

"You have to get them out or he will kill them." Michelle pleaded with Jordan every day since the horrific showdown. She knew Colin's death sealed their fate.

The health care team Jordan assembled was instrumental in Michelle's quick progress. Their care allowed her to recover enough to handle some tough questions by the task force.

"What's the status?" Jordan asked at the latest briefing with Special Agent Fisher that took place at the police station down town. Undercover agents had infiltrated the compound. The new intel, along with Michelle's help, escalated timeline of the operation.

"We've confirmed all are safe. The young girl identified as Madison, the young boy identified as Tommy, and Olivia identified as the matriarch of the house, have not been moved from their original location," Special Agent Fisher said.

"That's good news."

"We are ready for the extraction phase. We are going in tonight. Once we get them out, we'll move them to an undisclosed location until it's safe to bring them to the ranch."

"What are their chances? Tell me straight."

"We have our best men on this. I'd say they have a ninety percent chance of coming out of this alive."

"That's not good enough, damn it. You have to do better than that, do you hear me?"

"Dante's cronies are the worst of the worst and have eyes and ears everywhere, but we're ready. We'll get them out. Taking Dante down, however, will be more complicated," Fisher said. "Go home and go about business as usual. You will be notified once we have them and they are secured."

Jordan headed back to the ranch. He was more convinced than ever that asking Maddie to marry him tonight was the right thing to do. If things didn't go well, he needed her to know that he'd be there for her and her entire family for the rest of his life.

Jordan entered the living room where Maddie, Michelle, and Ally huddled on the plush sofa wrapped in blankets with cups of sweet tea.

"Maddie, could I speak with you for a moment?"

"Yes, sure. Of course." She sensed he was anxious, but could not get a complete read on him. *Watch her?* She signaled to Ally as she walked around the back of the sofa so Michelle could not see her.

Ally nodded and Michelle didn't notice their exchange.

Jordan helped Maddie up the stairs with a careful touch to her lower back as if she were made of porcelain. His eyes were open and the world was a different place. He saw the life he wanted, one he could have had nine years ago and gave away because of his own stupidity and fear. She was his precious center.

"Come, sit," he said, his hand guided her to her bed.

"What's wrong?" she asked. The intense look on his chiseled face sent a chill down her spine.

"Nothing is wrong." Both of his knees hit the floor in front of her, her feet hung in the air on the edge of the high mattress.

He caressed her soft arms and parted her legs so he could move in closer to the edge of the bed.

"Come here." He brought her lips to his. With a light touch of his bottom lip, he captured its tenderness.

Something was different about *them*. About *him*. A good kind of different. An unexpected special and amazing kind of different.

"I have something I want to ask you." He took a deep breath. "I don't know how I ever let you go. I was young. Selfish. Foolish." He looked down at her delicate, perfect hands. "I don't want to live one day without you. You've captured my soul. I am yours. I've always been yours. I'll always be yours. Please be mine. Forever. Will you marry me?"

His eager, light brown eyes stared into hers. He never felt more exposed, more vulnerable. When she didn't answer right away, he felt like his body had floated into an abyss with no way out.

After a short pause that seemed like years, she gave her answer.

"Yes. A thousand times, yes." The embrace that followed felt as magical as any fairy tale could. "I have something I want to tell you too. I was afraid of how you'd react. I was searching for the right time, but I think *now* is the time."

"What is it?"

She cupped his strong jaw in her hands; the tremble made his teeth chatter. She moved his face toward hers and revealed her secret. "We are going to have a baby."

"What? Really?" He picked her up and squeezed her as tightly as her could without crushing her ribs.

"Are you happy?" She was certain she didn't misinterpret his reaction, but wanted to hear him say it.

"Am I happy? I have never been happier than I am at this very moment. I'll give you anything you want. If you want to start your own law practice here, I'll set that up for you. If you want to stay home, run the house, and have babies, I'll help you do that too."

"I just want you. All of you. All the time," she answered. "And I do want us to have a big family, lots of kids."

"You've got it. Twenty kids or more." He threw his hands into the air in a delirious tangent.

"Whoa, cowboy. That might be a little too ambitious," she said. "We should keep this between us, just until we get Madison back."

"I knew you'd say that and I agree, mostly."

"Mostly?"

"I told Ally I was going to ask you."

"You did?" She gave him a punch to his massive shoulder.

"I did." He laughed as he flashed a mischievous smile. "I wanted her to know because I asked her to move here to Timberton, with us."

"Really, Jordan?"

"She's been an incredible friend to you. I wanted to give you another incentive to leave New York for good and move back home, here with me, just in case I wasn't enough of an incentive for you." He braced himself for another punch.

The grandfather clock in the downstairs hallway struck midnight. Jordan took a walk downstairs to check things out. Michelle was restless, but managed to fall asleep on the couch during the movie while Ally chatted on her phone. She called all her new friends in town to let them know her plans to move to Timberton permanently.

Just as he was about to pick Michelle up off the couch and carry her upstairs, Jordan's cell phone rang. It was Roger. "This better be good news," he said aloud before he answered the call.

"Roger. Talk to me." He walked into the other room for some privacy.

"Good news and bad news."

"What is it?"

"The team got them out. All three of them."

"Thank God."

"But, Dante's men discovered they were gone almost immediately. We don't know how they found out so fast. The agents didn't get much of a head start."

"Damn it!" Jordan flared with anger, venom seeped from his pores.

"Our guys on the inside said Dante's unhinged. He's coming after them and then he's coming after Michelle. You are all in serious danger."

Jordan slammed the phone down on the table, the call still connected. Roger talked to no one for a few minutes before he realized he was talking to himself. Jordan did a thorough check of the security system and the cameras that monitored every possible entrance and exit in and out of the ranch while he alerted the security team to the latest threat.

If that evil son of a bitch thinks he's going to hurt my family again, he's a damn fool. The feds had better find him or I will.

He rushed to the basement to unlock a secret room filled with an arsenal of weapons he'd collected over the years to protect his land and prize-winning horses. His stash of long-range shotguns, semiautomatic handguns, and an endless supply of ammunition were at the ready.

"If you come anywhere near us," he said with his 9mm cocked, "you're a dead man."

CHAPTER SIXTEEN

Jordan bolted from the hallows of his sanctuary-turned-hostile-fortress. His steel-toe boots hit the stairs with meaningful steps that echoed into the kitchen as if a stampede of wild boar escaped from the basement.

"Ally, get Michelle upstairs now." His knuckles turned red with the force of his grip.

"No! Stop!" Michelle wouldn't let anyone touch her.

"Honey, it's just me. It's Ally. Wake up, sweetie. You're safe. It's okay." Jordan is going to carry you upstairs now."

She woke up in imminent fear. Unaware of her safe surroundings, she lashed out at the kind voice and scratched Ally's face with a claw-like fist, flesh from her porcelain skin left under Michelle's fingernails. Ally's blood dripped in thin rows of four.

"Fuck!" The sting, both physical and emotional, took Ally off guard.

"Come with me," Jordan said. He grabbed Ally and took her to Miss Camilla's room so she could apply first aid and stop the bleeding. "She'll take care of you. I'll be right back. You'll be okay. Michelle doesn't know where she is."

"I know. It's fine. Just go to her." She waved her hand.

"You're a good person, Alicia Carter."

"Yeah. I know." She shrugged off her injury. "This is nothing compared to what she went through. Go to her. She needs you."

Jordan approached Michelle with caution and a haze remained in her eyes. The psychiatrist Jordan hired to watch over her warned them all of the horrific flashbacks, dreams, and deep depression that would surface for years to come.

"Michelle?" he said as he touched her forehead. "Do you know who I am? Will you let me take you upstairs to see your sister?"

"Jordan?" She shook her head to rid herself of the fog.

"Yes, it's me. You are safe. Dante won't hurt you anymore. I promise you."

She buried her head in his chest without a word. He lifted her with ease and carried her upstairs to her bed. It was as if she was in a trance. No sound, no movement, no soul inside her frail body. She seemed to slip into a catatonic state.

"I'm going to call the doctor." Jordan filled Maddie in on her behavior and Ally's injury.

"Yes, call right away." She cradled her sister in her arms and wrapped her in the soft, rose-colored blanket that lay at the foot of her king-size bed. Maddie's instinct to nurture would never be limited again.

"Doctor, this is Jordan Kingston. Could you please call me asap? I need you to come and look at Michelle. She's showing the signs you warned us to watch out for. Call me." Jordan placed his phone in the side leg pocket of his jeans. "I'll let you know what she says when she calls me back."

Maddie nodded. "Could you please crack the window open a bit?"

"Sure."

"We will have an amazing life once all this is behind us," she said as she watched him reach up high, careful to slide the curtain open without disturbing the design. The moonlight bounced off his magnificent frame; the V-shape of his back flared with each stretch.

"It will all be behind us soon. No more regrets."

"I love you," she said.

"My dear, sweet Madison," he said with a swagger that drew her in. "I love *you*." He closed the door behind him with finesse. She felt a piece of her leave the room with him.

"Miss Camilla? How's your patient?" Jordan went to check on their new roommate.

"She's got some good scratches here, but not too deep."

"You okay?" He shifted toward Ally to hear her answer.

"I'm fine. How are my girls doing upstairs? Do you need me to do anything for them tonight?"

"No, thanks though. I'm waiting for a call back from the doctor."

"That's a good idea." She pushed herself off the kitchen stool. "I'm gonna head up to bed now. Come get me if you need me, okay?"

"Will do."

Half an hour passed. Jordan checked the camera footage and made sure his men were sharp and ready for the worst at this late hour.

"Doctor?" Jordan answered his phone before it could ring twice.

"Yes, I retrieved your message. How's Michelle doing?"

"Not well. She slipped into some kind of trance-like state. It's like she's not here with us, not in her body or something. She had a pretty bad nightmare and scratched the hell out of a friend who woke her up."

"What was the nightmare about?"

"I don't know exactly. We didn't want to press it. We put her to bed and I called you."

"That's good. Okay. I will be over first thing in the morning. But I will tell you that, in my opinion, reuniting her with her daughter is key here. She has experienced unimaginable trauma. The long-term effect on a person who has endured the kind of abuse she suffered, and for such a long period, could be delayed for months or even years. An individual's personal experience has a profound effect on their response to the treatment and recovery. In her case, without her daughter by her side, I believe she will slip further away from us."

"Oh, fuck," he answered, filters off. "Sorry. I apologize. I didn't mean to be disrespectful."

"It's quite all right. I know this is a difficult situation."

"Thank you, doctor."

Jordan knew what he had to do. "Hey. Wake up. We have a problem." Jordan summoned Roger at all hours and tonight was no exception.

He knew that if Jordan called, he'd better pick up no matter what time of day or night.

"What's wrong?" He threw the covers off and sat to attention on the side of his bed.

"We have to change the plan."

"What do you mean?"

"We can't wait for the team to bring down Dante before we bring Michelle's daughter here."

"That would be a big mistake. Too early to move them. The two of them in the same location? Not a good idea."

"Maybe, but we have no choice. Michelle's very mentally ill. The doctor thinks she's slipping away from us. He said the trauma was so severe for so long that the only way to keep from losing her might be to reunite her with her daughter."

"Might be?"

"Damn it, Roger! We have no choice, we have to try."

"Okay," Roger answered as he grabbed the top of his head to keep it from detaching from his shoulders. "Let me get on this and see how fast we can move them. I'll need to get a real time update of Dante's location. My guy on the inside will be checking in around an hour from now."

"Good. Get on it."

Sleep was not an option. Failure was not an option. Jordan stood in front of the cameras the rest of the night and watched each frame. Each and every image formed a permanent imprint in his mind.

At 6:00 a.m., Jordan saw Roger's old vehicle approaching the gate. He signaled his team to check and make sure it was Roger, alone, in the vehicle, and then let him through.

As he drove up the private road, Jordan directed him to pull his car over to the side of the house so it wouldn't block the entrance to the front door. When Roger stepped out of the car, he looked pale and panicked.

"What's going on?" Jordan asked.

"Here the skinny." Roger jumped right in, one hand on each hip and a brief glance at the gravel. "The word is Dante wants Michelle eliminated. He's doesn't want to risk her talking. She knows too much. Just like we thought, as long as Dante had their daughter to use as leverage against her, he was sure she'd never talk. But now that we have Madison, he wants Michelle dead."

"We have to get that son of a bitch once and for all. He's the one who's gonna be dead!" Jordan punched the hood of Roger's old jalopy.

"Look. We have to be smart here." Roger's open hand a made a formidable stop sign. "I explained the circumstances to Commander McFarley, the leader of this operation. He doesn't like it, but he'll prepare his men to move Olivia, Tommy, and Madison in an unmarked car within twenty-four hours. Not that you need it, but we'll transfer all agents to this location. You have an army here already, but with Dante's goons everywhere, extra men can't hurt."

"Let's do it. Let's bring them home. We got this."

"Let's hope so." Roger shook his head with doubt.

Michelle's decline was imminent. At 9:00 a.m. sharp the doctor arrived, assessed her condition and administered some medication to keep her comfortable.

"How she's doing?" Jordan asked as the doctor exited the bedroom.

"Michelle is extremely weak and in a state of panic. She's is falling into a deep depression and experiencing crippling feelings of guilt for leaving her daughter even though she had no choice. But I will say, her coping skills up until now have been nothing short of miraculous. That poor girl has been through hell."

"What should we do for her?"

"Get her daughter back." The doctor turned away and headed down the grand staircase without another word.

For the remainder of the day, Maddie stayed by Michelle's side with the hope that the medication would keep her from slipping further away while Jordan coordinated with Commander McFarley and his team to finalize the plan to bring everyone home.

The commander ordered a complete sweep of all roads and wooded areas that led to the ranch from the holding location right before the departure.

"Scheduled departure is 0200 hours sir." Special Agent Vortan gave the commander a final update.

"Excellent. We have one hour until go time," Commander McFarley answered. "Special Agent Vortan, all agents are to use the secure channel at all times. I don't have to remind you of the sensitive information transmitted here. No leaks. No mistakes. Is that clear?"

"Yes, sir."

Jordan and his team had access to the secure frequency and listened in.

"All units, agents, and personnel stand by," the commander said.

Only minutes left before the car was scheduled to leave the holding location, tensions ran high and the danger was palpable. No matter how prepared or how clever the agents were in protecting the innocent from vicious criminals like Dante, Olivia, Tommy and Madison's lives were about to be put in grave danger.

With no further ado, Commander Farley's final order disseminated at 0200 hours.

"Prepare for departure in three...two... one. Execute departure."

The plain black car driven by Special Agent Baldwin left on its mark and carried the three innocent targets along with Special Agent Vortan for extra security.

"All is a go. I repeat, it's a go." Jordan wished he felt as confident as the commander sounded.

"Miss Olivia, I'm scared," Madison said.

Tommy's sleeping head burrowed into Olivia's belly.

"Don't worry dear," she answered, a firm hug and a kiss on the head proved to be settling. "We are going to see your mommy now. We'll be there soon. These men are giving us a nice ride. Isn't that right?" Olivia spoke loud enough for the men to hear.

"Yes, of course," Special Agent Vortan said with a full turn of his head to look at the children and make them feel more comfortable.

"I think you're nice." Sweet Madison's voice echoed against the cold steel safety bars.

"Well, thank you, young lady. I don't get to hear that too often."

Olivia did her best not to show fear, but as the time ticked away, her nerves got the best of her. "How much longer?" she asked, a heavy dose of panic apparent in her voice.

"Not much longer, ma'am. Should be about another fifteen minutes."

"It's very dark out tonight." Olivia made conversation to break the eerie silence, but included a riddle with a purpose. "No moonlight at all. Barely a street light. How do you know what's lurking out there?"

"I think I know what you're asking, ma'am. We know. Rest assured. We are the best at what we do." His answer was just vague enough so the children would not understand.

"That's good to hear." She was relieved, but not convinced.

The entrance to the ranch was in sight. Special Agent Baldwin engaged the secure line to announce their arrival. "Lead vehicle twenty yards away."

"I see you." An unfamiliar, male voice answered.

"Agent, please identify yourself," Baldwin asked. "I repeat. Agent, identify yourself."

Silence was the only reply.

"Abort!" Commander McFarley gave the command over the hacked line with no hesitation. "Abort!"

"What's happening?" Olivia became panic-stricken. She wrapped the children in her arms as if hell had descended upon them.

"Get down." Special Agent Vortan ordered them lower their bodies as far as they could. The children cried amidst the confusion. "Someone has hacked the frequency."

The car turned at a fierce pace to head back in the other direction when Special Agent Vortan saw a red laser dot on Olivia's back as she prayed aloud and lay on top of the children, her body a human shield.

"Shit, Baldwin. Swerve. Sharp right! Swerve. Now!"

Baldwin didn't ask any questions and did as he was told.

A shot fired from the dark wooded area not twenty feet from the gate. The bullet would have hit Olivia square in her back if it weren't for the bullet-proof vehicle that protected them.

"What the fuck!" Baldwin said. He ducked and lifted his shoulders to meet his ears. "Where did that come from?"

⟞⊹ ⊹⟝

Jordan heard every word. In a rage, he called Roger. "Get hold of Baldwin and Vortan on the other line he had set up and tell them to bring the car to the remote stables on the far side of the property. You know where they are. My men are there and ready. Do it now."

Without giving Roger a chance to answer, Jordan jumped into his car to meet them at the remote stables with semiautomatic rifle in hand and his 9mm Glock secured to his backside.

The caravan shifted direction and made the two-mile ride around the perimeter of the property while Roger navigated the course using the other line. As the caravan approached the final three-quarter mile mark, he directed them to take a right turn into what looked like a typical cluster of evergreen trees minding their own business on the edge the main road.

"Turn into the woods on your right hand side right before you pass the small, green house with the white picket fence," Roger said. "You'll see a narrow dirt road. Drive half a mile in. Take a left at the yellow shed and follow that road another half a mile. You'll come to an open field. The stables are on your left."

"Got it." Special Agent Vortan answered as the car bounced from left to right. The tires tore up the ground and left a pitted dirt trail in its wake. "There." He pointed to the yellow shed. "Turn here."

The dirt road was pitch black with nothing but headlights to guide the car through the thick brush.

Jordan arrived at the stables well ahead of the others and parked his car behind the large concrete back wall of the building that housed heavy equipment used to landscape the property. Six headlights approached and stopped on a dime as Jordan emerged from the shadows.

"Special Agent Vortan here." He identified himself upon exiting the passenger side of the car and flashed his badge.

"Let's get them out of here. My men are surrounding the area. Now that they are inside the perimeter, they'll be safe. No one will get past my team." Jordan's presence needed no introduction. He opened the rear door on the passenger side to bring Tommy and Madison to safety.

"Olivia, hand me the children," he asked with an unmistakable purpose.

Olivia gave the crying children a gentle assist and guided them in Jordan's direction.

Agent Baldwin emerged from the driver's seat, swung open the rear door of the car, and pulled Olivia out with a force that dislocated her left shoulder.

"You're not going anywhere." Olivia was unable to move her small frame an inch. The cold barrel of his gun indented the side of her face as he pressed it against her temple. "Give me the girl or I will blow her pretty little head right off."

"Okay, I'm listening," Special Agent Vortan answered, his hands held up high to show his cooperation.

"I want the girl."

"You know I can't do that." Vortan glanced at the children. Madison's face was buried in Jordan's left thigh, Tommy's face planted in his right hip.

"Put the gun down and I can help you get out of whatever mess you're in," Vortan said.

"You can't help me. Give me the girl. I'm not gonna ask you again." Olivia let out a shrill scream of horror that could shatter glass.

"Shut up!" Baldwin pushed the steel barrel into her temple farther than before. The imprint he left in her flesh was no match for the imprint that would remain in her memory forever.

"Look up, you corrupt son of bitch. You'll never get out of here alive." Jordan pointed to the sniper at the top of the concrete wall that had Baldwin's forehead square in its crosshairs.

"I know right now you think you can't get out of this mess, but there is a way. Let me help you. Don't do this," Vortan said. "You don't want to hurt her. I know you, Baldwin. Think of the boy. She's his mother."

"Shut up. That's not my problem." Baldwin's anger escalated. Her death was imminent.

"Not your problem? Well *this* is your problem." Jordan reached behind his back and before anyone could react, his arm stretched across the roof of the car. His long reach brought his 9mm within six feet of Baldwin's face. "Your time is up. Let her go or you're a dead man."

Baldwin pushed Olivia to the ground, her ribs cracked by the rocks that broke her fall. In a split second, the barrel of Baldwin's gun swung from Olivia to his temple. With a pull of the trigger, he sent a bullet clear through to the other side of his skull. Carnage and blood flew in every direction.

"Oh, shit!" Vortan could not believe what just happened.

"Vortan, move. Get Olivia and bring her to my car. Kids. Come now. Everybody's all right." Jordan picked up the children as if they were weightless and used his body to block their view of the dead man lying only a few feet away.

Olivia climbed into Jordan's vehicle, pushing the kids ahead of her.

"Olivia, you're going to be all right," Jordan said as she huddled with the children in the back seat, every bone in her body shaking at once. "I'm going to get you some help."

Olivia cried for herself and for the children on the dark ride back; her heart pounded faster than it ever had. The sight of the stadium-like structure calmed her and she knew they were close to safety.

"Mr. Kingston, I never thought I'd see my friend again."

"I wasn't going to let anything happen to any of you."

Even through the darkness, the palatial home lit up her sad eyes. It was heaven on earth, the kind of place she'd dreamed of and had seen only once in a magazine.

"Let's go in and get you looked at by a doctor." Jordan helped her out of the back seat as she winced in pain from her broken ribs.

"I'd like to see Michelle first, sir. If I may?"

"Only if you call me Jordan," he said with a kindness that made her feel right at home.

"Jordan. Yes, I might need some time to get that right." Her light giggle was forceful enough to cause her to grab her side in agony.

Camilla opened the front door.

"Miss Camilla, this is Olivia, Tommy, and Michelle's daughter, Madison." Jordan picked Madison up and placed her on his muscular forearm. Her little legs dangled; her tattered shoes tugged at his heart.

Miss Camilla could not hold back her tears. "I'm so delighted to meet you all. Please," she said as she waved them into the living room and out of the foyer. "Come in. Be at home."

"Your home is so beautiful," Olivia said in awe of her new surroundings. "Children, can we say thank you to…Jordan." She felt proud to please him.

"No need to thank me," Jordan said. "You are always welcome here."

"Very well." She nodded with respect.

"Would you like to see your mom?" Jordan asked Madison who was content to stay perched on his forearm.

"Yay! Mommy!" She threw her small arms into the air.

"Let's go. Everyone follow me." He walked up the grand staircase with Madison secured in his embrace.

Jordan knows the danger is not over with Dante still at large. Now that everyone is secure within the walls of the guarded ranch, he can execute his plan to put an end to him and ensure the safety of everyone he loves. Today, he will stay home with his family, but tomorrow Dante will wish he never crossed his path.

Miss Camilla and Tommy assisted Olivia in the ascent. Tommy showed maturity beyond his young years as he held his mother's hand and paused with her on every step.

"She's in this room over here." Jordan pointed to the half open door with a hand-painted plaque that read *My Home and My Heart is Where You Are.*

With his free hand, he opened the door and stepped in first. Maddie jumped up silently at the sight of her precious family, a sight she was not certain she would see again.

Within seconds, Michelle awoke. It was as if she knew her daughter had entered the room. Even the heavy dose of medication did not keep her sedated.

A wishing well of tears turned to a stream that watered each flower on her cotton nightgown, the pure joy hindered only by her disbelief that this moment was true. Her arms, weak and limp from the medication, stretched out with every bit of life left in her to grab her daughter and never let her go.

"Sweetheart, here is your mom." Jordan said to the angel whose face remained planted in his shoulder." He carried her to Michelle and placed her on her chest with care.

The moment was surreal. Peace and hope took the place of fear and despair.

"Thank you, God." Michelle rejoiced. She rocked her daughter back and forth as Madison's touch turned her flesh from chalky white to rosy pink.

"She's coming back to us," Maddie said. She looked up at Jordan with her hand against her mouth, overcome by the miracle she just witnessed and the promise of their new life.

Jordan took Maddie's palm, gave it a gentle kiss, and circled his heart with her whole hand. "You'll always be my girl. I promise you...forever."